FOREVER SHE

(TALES OF OTHERWORLDLY LOVE & PASSION)

AMITAV GANGULY

DEDICATED TO MY FAMILY FOR THEIR UNSTINTED SUPPORT,
ALWAYS!

Contents

CHAPTER ONE

OBSESSION FOR WHOM?

That day, I descended from the train on the uneven stretch of the platform of a small station in the Santhal Pargana division of the State of Jharkhand.

It was a winter afternoon, the time was 4.45 p.m., and the sun was playing on the platform. While shielding the gleams of the sun with my open right palm, I shivered as the freezing wind blew through the adjoining lush green forest a little away from the station. Then I looked around; no one was moving except for a few rail workers. Knowing that a man should be there to receive me and not find him, I picked up my small suitcase and started walking towards the exit gate through the tiny building.

Coming out of the rickety gate of the station, which was a certain distance from the building, I again conducted a reconnaissance of the region. The prominent sight was the tall green forest directly in front of me, albeit a few hundred yards ahead, the expanse of which was at all sides beyond my vision. At the foot of the forest lay a single-track tar road accessible from that gate and ran parallel to the station boundary, towards the left and the right.

I took only a few moments to register, and then my eyes searched for that man I was told would meet me. His name was Khagen Das, and he was the local coordinator for the forest survey duty I was assigned to do here.

But at that time, there was nobody as far as I could see, which was surprising since he had confirmed to Mr Shivaganga Gupta, my boss, at the head office in Ranchi two days earlier that he would personally come and pick me up from the station. That was needed because there was virtually no public transport from the station near the village due to sparse traffic. People preferred to walk in this part of the country, and if they wanted transport, a few cycle rickshaws would probably be available.

However, my destination was not the village but a government circuit house situated in another direction, about three kilometers inside the forest. The destination was away from the regular route, not usually visited by the locals, so Khagen Das needed to come with his own transport and take me to the circuit house.

Almost 15 minutes had since passed, and still, there was no sign of him. I knew he had a mobile phone and tried to reach him, but there was poor connectivity, and my calls failed repeatedly.

By that time, I walked back towards the station building within its boundary and, finding a concrete bench outside the structure, sat on it in a contemplative mood. I could not decide my next step if Khagen failed to come. It was not that I had the option of going back since I had come to this remote place on government duty. And even if I thought of returning, I could not do so immediately since I was aware that the next train to Ranchi was a day later.

As I thought glumly, I realised that the winter sun was setting fast, darkness was creeping in, and the rural area's chill quickly became unbearable. When I boarded the train, I was told there was rain during the past week, so today's cold had a wet feeling.

About half an hour had elapsed, I had become terribly restless and seriously thinking about walking to the village to find a way out, as the station staff also could not be of any help, when I heard a cycle rickshaw enter through the gate and came to a halt a little distance away from where I was sitting.

Khagen came down from the rickshaw seat with an apologetic attitude.

He was a short young man with a robust physique and muscular arms. His appearance was noticeable with a weather-beaten mongoloid feature, having curly and well-oiled black hair, wearing a well-pressed white cotton shirt and trousers. Being an educated and efficient man, he was expected to support me in my government duties next week.

"Sorry, sir!" He said, his voice was thick and seemed to be suiting his personality.

"I have been waiting for more than an hour; at least you should have informed me over my mobile phone that you will be late," I responded with slight irritation.

"Sir, I was with the local police about the disappearance of a young Adivasi woman; I know her well, and the police thought that I could be of some help." Saying this, Khagen picked up my suitcase and lodged it inside the rear part of the cycle rickshaw and invited me to take a seat there; then, getting up, he sat next to me with some difficulty since it was quite narrow and hard.

As we took the road towards the forest, the sun disappeared behind the jungle, but there was sufficient light to proceed. Khagen said we would reach within the next half an hour before complete darkness set in. There would not be much difficulty even otherwise as this road had temporary streetlights until the circuit house, which also had an electricity connection.

We moved in silence, gradually hearing various noises of insects and small animals emanating from the wooded area.

"Sir, once we reach there, you will find the accommodation at the circuit house a little old but comfortable; please settle in. An aged Adivasi man, Pandu Mahato, lives there; he is the caretaker cum attendant, a cook, who will be available at all times during your stay and take good care of you." Khagen said after a few minutes to break the silence.

"What is the story about that Adivasi woman you said has disappeared?" I was slightly curious in the absence of any other conversation topic at that time.

"This incident happened about ten days ago. That woman, Mahua Mahato, daughter of Pandu Mahato, has many admirers and perhaps one or two serious lovers. We think she has eloped with some man and would soon get in touch with her father or return on her own. Even if she does not, that will not be surprising as this type of 'missing girls' has happened in many other villages. Anyway, the police think fit to start an investigation." Khagen replied.

I nodded absent-mindedly; my thoughts were focused on the government duties I had to perform from tomorrow for which I came to this God-forsaken place. But I also reflected on how Pandu Mahato could take good care of me if he were upset by his daughter's disappearance.

Soon we turned right directly into the deep forest. The evening light was such that I could still see the expanse mainly covered with towering sal, neem, and banyan trees, which, along with shrubs and bushes, virtually made the forest look like a solid mass; more so with creeping plants intertwined around thick tree trunks and the ground below being copiously covered with fallen leaves and other debris of those trees. As the darkness gradually set in, the volume of forest noise increased. The narrow tar road we were travelling, lined by occasional streetlights, dimly lit, cut through the forest in a meandering fashion.

After about fifteen minutes, we saw a relatively vast clear area ahead on the right side of the road at the center of which the circuit house was located; it was an old fashioned, medium-sized bungalow with extended French windows having a low green square hedge around it with a wooden gate in the front. There was a tiny structure outside the hedge on the right side, presumably for the caretaker. There were four wooden lampposts alongside the hedge of the circuit house, each on an individual corner. The clear area in front of the building, beyond the gate, had the uneven ground covered with dead leaves, although there were no trees in the immediate vicinity; the winds could be shifting the leaves there.

Seeing us, an old man, very dark-skinned with a shocking maze of white hair, slightly bent, wearing dhoti and kurta, hurried towards us with folded hands. His face was expressionless.

"Sir, this is Pandu Mahato, your caretaker about whom I told you. He speaks very little but will take care of you with dedication. Please do not ask him anything about his missing daughter. He will definitely break down and leave us." Khagen said.

Pandu bowed before me, picked up my suitcase, and walked towards the gate. Khagen fished into his bulging front shirt pocket, where he had kept a wad of notes and loose coins, took some money out with difficulty, and paid off the rickshaw puller. Then, turning towards me, he smiled and said, "Please make yourself comfortable for the night; I will ask Ramnath Sapru, the survey supervisor, to come tomorrow morning for your work."

"Where do you stay? How will you go now?" I asked.

"About a kilometer towards the north from here. I will walk through the forest; there is a regular path through it." He pointed at the rear forest of the circuit house and switched on a torch which he took out from his trouser pocket.

After settling down in my room post a simple but tasty dinner, I relaxed. The bedroom was extensive with a high ceiling and tall French windows at the head side of a double-sized ornate bed and an absolutely bare white wall at the foot side of the bed; other furniture consisted of a bedside table, another round table a little away, two high backed cushioned chairs and an elaborate chest of drawers. The bathroom was attached, and there were two doors, one for entry into the room and the other for the bathroom.

As I lay on the bed with a cigarette to my lips, staring at the ceiling, I was thinking aimlessly about the journey, duties I had to attend to from tomorrow, and the case of that missing young woman, Mahua Mahato. What could have happened to her?

As I felt sleepy and switched off the light, my eyes casually focused on the bare white wall before me at the foot of the bed and noticed that a large rectangular spotlight was falling on it, coming in through the French window from the lamppost light situated outside alongside the hedge. There was nothing more to see, so I turned around and fell asleep.

The following day was a glorious sunny day; Ramnath Sapru, the survey supervisor, a short and non-descriptive man, came, and after breakfast, I immersed myself in my duties, which took almost three hours of continuous attention. As, later, we casually spoke about the missing woman, he appeared unnaturally unsympathetic and said such women of lax morals could very well meet gory ends.

When the time was past one o'clock in the afternoon, Pandu informed us that the lunch was ready.

After I had completed my lunch and was sitting, with a cigarette, in an old-fashioned easy chair on the open verandah of the circuit house, I saw a police jeep reach the gate, and a tall, clean-shaven uniformed man with very short dark hair, got down and walked towards me.

He introduced himself as Sub-Inspector Nick Dev and informed that he was carrying out the investigation of missing Mahua.

I responded, "I am Khepri Pal, and I have come here from Ranchi to do a forest survey of this area. Can I be of any assistance?"

He smiled and said, "Sir, basically, I have come to speak to the father of Mahua Mahato, but I am glad to have met you. Let me interrogate Pandu Mahato, after which I will come and have afternoon tea with you."

When he returned, we spoke about the case with two cups of tea before us. Although I was a disinterested party, he was a friendly man and seemed happy to know and talk to me.

"Sir, Mahua is a young woman of about 22 years, intelligent, a first-class commerce graduate, and friendly with almost everyone in the village. As is normal at this age, she is close to some young men, particularly a fellow named Bir Bhadra, with rumours of a one-sided romantic alliance. That man is a womaniser. When I interrogated him, he could say nothing except that the last he met Mahua was a day before her disappearance, and at that time, she was perfectly normal. But I do not believe him; he is my prime suspect. I have been asking around others too but unable to get any leads."

Somehow, I became curious to know more about this young woman. "Do you have any picture of this missing woman?" I asked.

Nick Dev nodded and took out a somewhat faded colour picture from his pocket, and handed it to me.

As I looked at the picture of a complete profile of Mahua, I sharply drew my breath in; she was dark-complexioned, gorgeous, with black wavy hair cascading up to her shoulders adorning a lotus-shaped face, with large kohled eyes, shapely lips, and a small nose with a pin. Flowers on the side of her hair were visible. She wore an ordinary pink saree with small prints, tightly wrapped around, with feet inserted into rubber sandals. Her hourglass figure would have shamed any international model. She was a villager who gave the impression to be, at the same time, rustic and trendy. Evidently, she was an educated and attractive woman, perhaps a rarity in this village.

She managed to fire my imagination in those moments like no female had done till then. I was not a school-going kid but a mature man who had seen 35 summers and had to deal with many women in various walks of life, some of them prettier than Mahua. But here, an intense sense of emotion flooded my consciousness. I felt that I should find and meet her as soon as possible. Who knew I might begin an affair with her if everything was positive? As these thoughts crossed my mind, I was a bit surprised, these were against my nature and personality, but I reckoned that I was a man with usual emotive and physical instincts; was I not?

Then mentally, I dithered! Oh my God! What was I thinking? Falling in love without actually seeing or meeting this young woman and that too within moments! And what would happen if I met her, asked for her love, and she refused?

I was indeed a one-of-a-kind foolish man! This was not love, at best temporary infatuation or is it a persistent obsession?

Soon, I controlled myself with a touch of cynicism and enquired, "What have you learnt by talking to her father now?"

"Well, he is of no help except telling us that fateful night she did not return here from the village where she had gone to make some purchases. She rode her bicycle and took the short path through the forest. At that time, the father got drunk, went to bed early, and was in a deep sleep for so long that he did not realise her absence until the next morning when he got up. He foolishly waited throughout the day without telling anyone, but she never returned. As days passed, and she remained absent, concerns were raised; the villagers searched for her all over this area, but that remained fruitless."

"What about her mother?"

"She died long ago. Mahua has no other family except her father."

"Are you searching the forest?"

"Yes, but it is a sizeable area and will take some time."

"What about her bicycle?"

"Even that is untraceable."

"Ramnath Sapru, who is working with me, has very negative views about the woman. Any idea?"

"Well, he is one of her admirers but was in his hometown, Dumka, when she disappeared. Perhaps he is bitter that he could not get her love."

"Do you think she ran away with someone?"

"Unlikely; otherwise, we would have found out by now."

"That means she could be dead?" I blurted out; I did not know why.

Sub-Inspector Nick Dev thought for some moments, "Maybe ...!"

I fervently hoped she was not; I wanted to meet her.

After a few civilities, the sub-inspector left.

Later in the night, as I prepared for bed after dinner, my mind was thoughtful. I knew that I had nothing to do with this case, but somehow, I seemed to get very much involved. More ever, my ever-increasing attraction for her appeared to be baffling.

Adding to my emotions, seeing her father doing his daily chores stoically even after such an unhappy incident made my heart go for him, although I kept myself away from discussions with him.

Soon, for some reason, I did not feel like retiring to bed and wrapping a dressing gown around me; I came out of the circuit house and slowly walked out of the gate to the clear area on the front, with a cigarette on my lips. Slight traces of winter fog stagnated in the atmosphere, but generally, the place was well lit with four wooden lampposts throwing yellow light around in a haze. The trees around the area seemed to stand tall, a little away like dark sentinels.

Strolling leisurely around, I returned to the circuit house and reached my bedroom. On the way, I noticed that Pandu Mahato had finished his work, switched off the kitchen light, and had already moved toward the tiny structure where he lived.

I did not know how long I had slept when suddenly my eyes flicked open. My sleep seemed to have evaporated in an instant. I frowned as generally; I was a deep sleeper. Turning, I picked up my radium wristwatch on the side table and found the time of 2.33 a.m.

Why the hell did I wake up?

I was about to go back to sleep when I noticed the large rectangular spotlight on the wall opposite me formed due to the light coming through the French window from the lamppost. Last night it was just a clear spotlight, but today I could see a clear dark shadow of a palm tree on it; the leaves were moving slightly in the wind. This was impossible; I had noticed that there was no tree anywhere near any lamppost.

What could it be?

I climbed out of my bed with some alacrity, walked towards the window, and peered out. There was nothing unusual. I could, of course, see that a strong wind was blowing, and the trees and leaves around the periphery of the clear area were swaying and moving. I also noticed the palm tree in question quite at a distance at the edge of the clear space on the far left; its leaves were also moving in the wind. The entire area was shrouded in semi-darkness, and the visibility was poor.

My sixth sense was telling me that this needed some investigation. I turned back from the window. There was no shadow of any tree on that rectangular spotlight by this time!

Again, I stepped out of the circuit house by opening its main door, walked out of the gate, and stood in the clear area, trying to focus on the palm tree, which I had already noticed did not have any lamppost near it.

There was some mystery about that tree, I was sure.

Without a second thought, I walked towards it, and on reaching below it, I paused; looking up and around, I could see nothing in the darkness. Then there was again a sudden gust of strong wind resulting in the dead leaves and tree droppings on the ground getting swept away, exposing the bare ground below. In fact, the land of around 25 feet in circumference below the palm tree became clean. Nothing unusual, but I found that the ground on which I was standing had loose soil, whereas the rest of the clean area had a hard floor.

I had my mobile phone with me, and switching on its torch, I could see the difference quite well. Still, nothing seemed abnormal, but I thought I would give it some thought tomorrow morning.

The following day, the sun was behind clouds, and fog still hung in the environment. Continuing the last night's weather, the cold wind also blew strongly, making the tall green trees rustle and sway perceptibly.

After finishing my work with the survey–supervisor, I thought for a long moment; that I was getting a hunch that I should talk to the sub-inspector.

He came soon with a team and met me.

"What you say is unbelievable, sir! But there is no harm in finding out what is buried under the loose soil. Most probably more soil."

When the police team started digging the loose ground under the palm tree, I was unsure what to expect.

Within a short time, after some vigorous digging till about two feet below, there was a shout from one of the excavators, "Sir, we see dark green coloured cloth pieces...."

And as the soil was moved away carefully, now, clearly, we could see the body of a woman, facing down, grotesquely positioned, her lengthy hair strewn and solidified in the soil; she was wearing a light green saree with a torn blouse, the saree was tattered, muddy and drawn up to her thighs, the legs were drawn together; her hands could not be seen since they were below the body which was in a slightly decomposed state with insects moving around. It was a ghastly sight!

Pandu Mahato, who witnessed this horrendous process, suddenly gave a cry, held his head with both hands, and sat down on the ground on his hunches.

"Mahua ... Mahua, what has happened to you...? Why am I alive to see this? What sin have I done? Why is God punishing me like this?" He started moaning and prostrated on the ground, curling up in a coma.

The dead woman's identity was not in doubt; she was Mahua Mahato!

Along with others, I helped her father go to his tiny structure. The police continued their procedure, and I returned to the circuit house.

While returning, my eyes were filled with tears; my emotions were severely shaken! This was atypical; I knew this woman had started an emotional upheaval in me when I first saw her photograph, but now, after seeing her end, her dead body, my feeling could not remain under control. It was as if I had lost my long-term lover!

But nobody should have any inkling of this; this was my secret and would die with me!

Soon, I called Mr Shivaganga Gupta, my boss, at the head office in Ranchi and gave him the details and the likelihood of the work getting delayed. He gave me permission to decide the best way forward. I tried to contact Khagen Das, but his mobile phone was switched off. Meanwhile, the villagers had learned about the discovery, and they arrived at that place in hordes. The police had a difficult time containing them.

An hour or so later, Sub-Inspector Nick Dev came inside the circuit house and met me. "Sir, I thank you for your help, but now we have to take this investigation forward. I will find out what exactly happened and who is the killer? I will keep you posted."

In the evening, Khagen Das arrived. "Sir, this is unthinkable! We have never seen this type of tragedy in these parts... I feel so sorry for her... I am sure the killer will be found."

Some changes in the arrangements had to be made; more specifically, another caretaker and cook were required since Pandu Mahato was severely traumatised and was taken to the local medical facility.

A couple of days had passed; it was a routine as I continued with my duties. But a severe depression was enveloping me throughout my waking hours!

The time was late in the afternoon when the sub-inspector arrived in his jeep and sat before me. I was studying a government report. Keeping aside the file, I looked at him inquiringly.

"Sir, let me tell you about the developments in this case. We got the autopsy done on an urgent basis, and it tells us that Mahua Mahato was brutally raped and then strangled to death. Very unfortunate! We have yet to pinpoint the killer, but we are working vigorously."

Upon hearing it, my throat withered; with a slight cough, I said, "Have you found anything?"

He shook his head slowly. "We have not been able to locate her bicycle or the spade used by the killer to dig the ground and bury her. As you know, we had rain recently, and the ground has become soft. However, there seems to be a clue ..., " he paused.

"What is it?" I leaned forward; I knew that I had become closely associated with this crime as never before.

"We found a ten-rupee coin in her grave. We do not know how it got there."

"Perhaps it belongs to the killer?" I opined.

"It makes no sense that the killer will throw a coin inside the grave after the crime."

"It must have fallen from his shirt pocket without realising it," I replied.

The sub-inspector stared at me for long moments. "That is possible, sir; we must check the fingerprints on that coin if that is feasible on such a small surface. And who could have kept money in his shirt pocket?"

Then a thought struck me, and I told him in detail, ending with, "In that case, first obtain the fingerprint of that man and compare it with that on the coin; we cannot charge anyone with rape and murder on mere suspicion."

I did not know that I could play a critical role in such a heinous crime investigation. It was not that I was willing to play such a role! The questions which disturbed me were:-

Did a supernatural prompting make me play that role? Who did that? Was that night's large rectangular spotlight on my bedroom wall, highlighting a palm tree's dark shadow although there was no such tree, happen to be such instigation? Whatever it might be, the result of that aberration galvanised me to act, go to the police so that justice could be delivered for an innocent young woman who had to give her life to a criminal lust!

Before those queries could be answered, it was essential to know the criminal's identity; here, I had already suspected and alerted the sub-inspector.

The next morning, I was with Sub-Inspector Nick Dev, who said that the man pointed by me was indeed the rapist-killer. The criminal was Khagen Das! In this society, nobody was beyond suspicion, especially for sex felonies, but the positivity was that justice also followed sporadically, at least it did here.

This crime's investigative facts were not far to seek; they only needed a keen sense of observation to understand. When I initially arrived at this place that evening with Khagen Das in a rickshaw, I had noticed that he paid the rickshaw puller by taking a wad of notes and some coins from his shirt pocket. I also saw that his pocket was literally bulging. So, it was not hard to guess that while committing the crime and in the ensuing struggle with Mahua Mahato, the tell-tale coin must have slipped out of his pocket and fallen on the ground and in the grave. Fortunately, he would have held that coin with his fingers at some point, so his impressions came on that. And during the investigation, his fingerprint on the coin matched. When he was confronted with these facts by the sub-inspector, he panicked and confessed. Mahua's bicycle and the spade were also recovered from the forest near Khagen Das's house.

The case was over, but the most inexplicable question remained to be answered. Who brought about this mysterious provocation?

It was not easy to reflect on this question, with a heart-wrenching trauma clouding my judgment!

Anyway, my government duty of almost 10 days ended, and I was scheduled to leave for Ranchi the next day.

As I lay on the bed that night looking at the large rectangular spotlight on the wall opposite me, thinking only about her, I suddenly found a dark shadow of unmistakably a woman gliding through it, only stopping for a moment. Getting up immediately, I went to the window and looked out; not that I expected to see anyone; but I understood from my sixth sense that Mahua Mahato's soul had emerged through her shadow. Now my incomprehensibility was getting cleared! It was she who initiated me to find her killer, and now it was she only who recognized my lending a hand. Why did she do that? Perhaps my love manifested itself to her for which she did all these; I would never know, ever!

CHAPTER TWO

LOVE FROM ETERNITY

Inspector Pyarelal Choubey, an obese short man with sweat dripping from his face, his uniform soggy and smelly, slammed his right fist on the bare wooden table. The interrogation room of the Kotwali Police station was windowless, bleak, and almost barren. Dhrupad Mandana, a man of medium built, non-descript face, cleanly shaven with ruffled hair sitting on a rickety metal chair at the side of the table, stared at the man before him apprehensively. It was apparent that the inspector was not satisfied with his replies. How could Dhrupad convince this unreasonable man about his innocence?

By the time Dhrupad got out of the dilapidated building, he felt really depressed. He was very upset about the course of the investigation and the police questioning. This was probably his thirteenth visit to this police station. The consequences of the twin tragedies of his beloved wife's death and to be suspected of such death were mind-boggling.

That Friday, in June, at 1.15 p.m., driving his Honda car, Dhrupad was keen to reach his office in the next 45 minutes. Fortunately, he arrived on time and at once was swamped with a string of meetings with customers in addition to his pending desk work.

Afterwards, thoroughly exhausted, he was returning home. It was just after 7.00 p.m. After a sharp shower during the late afternoon, the city traffic was at its worst. As he negotiated his car through a particularly narrow stretch with the crumbling road, he became aware that his mobile phone was buzzing. Picking it up from the adjoining seat, he peered at it. The call was from his home landline. As the word 'Home' appeared on his mobile phone display screen, he was jerked out of his boredom of the last one hour of slow driving.

"How is it possible?" he thought, "there is nobody at home." He knew that Sweta, his younger sister, who could have been at home, had visited her friend across the city and was not expected till tomorrow afternoon.

He still took that call.

"Yes, who are you? What do you want?"

There was no response, and doubt was creeping in him that something was wrong.

He waited for some seconds and interjected with a higher note, "Who is that? Why are you not replying?" There was still no response. With a tinge of concern, he hollered into the instrument, "What is happening? Hell!"

As he waited in vain for a reply, he feared that somebody had gone into his flat and there could be mischief somewhere.

Disconnecting the line, he called Sweta. She was prompt in taking his call, and when Dhrupad told her about the strange call, she sounded worried, "Why are you not calling Mrs Dhamija?" She has the duplicate keys to our flat; she can check out and call you back." It was a good suggestion since her flat was just across from Dhrupad's flat.

When contacted, Mrs Dhamija was extremely helpful. "Certainly, I will find out, Dhrupad."

A little later, she returned his call. Her voice sounded doubtful. "The door of your flat is padlocked from the outside in addition to the built-in lock. There is nobody around. What can be the problem?"

When Dhrupad reached his 10th floor flat about 30 minutes later, he was somewhat worried. Opening the door, he entered and looked around with trepidation. Everything seemed perfectly normal. The landline telephone instrument on the sideboard next to the dining table was precisely on the same spot he remembered it was, and even the thin coat of dust was untouched.

Eventually, dismissing the incident as some technical glitch in the telephone exchange, he changed into his pyjamas and, wrapping his dressing-gown, went into the kitchen to make a cup of tea. After putting the milk in the pan to boil, he went back to the living room to pick up the newspaper he had not read in the morning.

Then, he observed that the landline telephone cable was disconnected from the wall socket and hanging loose behind the sideboard. Wondering who could have done this, he swiftly moved forward, picked up the cable to check, and found no dial tone. It was clear, but not how a telephone call could go to him from that dead instrument, or did someone call him and subsequently unplug the cable?

Reconnecting the cable, he slowly walked back and sat on the sofa. It had escaped his mind entirely that the milk was boiling in the kitchen by then. A few minutes had gone by when suddenly remembering it, he rushed to the kitchen to switch off the gas burner. But the gas was already closed. Who had done that?

The realisation then hit him that something was definitely wrong somewhere. He gulped as fear overwhelmed him; nevertheless, he prepared his tea, carried the cup back to the sofa, and kept it on the centre table. His hands were shaking lightly.

He had lost count of the time he was sitting on the sofa when this trance was shattered by his mobile phone ringing. The phone display showed that the call was from Sweta, but there was no response when he took the call. Thinking that there could be some connectivity problem, he disconnected and called her back.

"No, I did not call you," she said. "In fact, I was thinking of doing that. What has happened? Any idea?" As Dhrupad narrated what had exactly occurred during the last more than an hour, she cried out, "Oh my God! Weird happenings! I am coming back immediately."

Dhrupad, feeling slightly relieved, leaned forward from his sofa to pick up the teacup, which he had forgotten; he assumed that the tea had become cold and would have to reheat it. However, it was not so; the tea was piping hot. He frowned; the weather was relatively warm at that time, and in any case, the tea would never have remained so hot for so long.

Was it another of these bizarre incidents?

His sixth sense told him that he might be in danger and had to escape from the flat.

Picking up the padlock and its key from the sideboard, he strode towards the main door. But another shock awaited him. As he attempted to open the door, he found it was not unlocking. He tried again, this time with greater force; still, it did not open. By now, he was sweating, his heart was pounding, and his mouth had turned dry in nervousness. He attempted to unbolt the door a few more times, but every time he failed. Had the built-in door lock broken?

At last, realising that any further effort would be futile, he staggered back on the sofa. A dark shroud of fear seemed to have wrapped him. He called Sweta again over her mobile phone, who was on her way and hoped to reach within the next three hours. She had the duplicate keys and asked him to keep calm.

Changing his mind about calling for any other help, he settled down to wait; still deeply apprehensive, he, however, felt that his eyes were closing; the day's exhaustion and strain on his emotions had literally drained his energies.

He was not sure whether it was sleep or he was losing his senses.

When he opened his eyes, the wall clock was striking the time of 10.00 p.m. He blinked and looked around, his mind was still a little fearful, but nothing was amiss anywhere. Thankfully by that time, his faculties had cleared. He felt in his bones that someone was trying to tell him something and confine him to his flat; the reason was not apparent.

He sat there thinking of what to do next.

An hour had passed, and Dhrupad was still in a contemplative mood when suddenly a faintly familiar scent of the perfume became discernible. He frowned and looked around; it was unclear how this could be possible. And then, strangely, a deluge of vivid memories started crossing through his consciousness like a vortex; he took one deep breath and closed his eyes again.

He began to think back!

Ravina, his dear wife, charming and beautiful, was the heart of the whirlpool of his memories. He recalled their relationship, which had a brief but hectic courtship, blooming into a passionate romance and concluding with their court marriage. And their union had brought so much happiness that it was a heavenly bliss; love was deep and reciprocal.

On the third day of their honeymoon in Mauritius, after their intense lovemaking, as she snuggled closer to him, she had whispered, "I am forever yours, Dhrupad, but do forgive me if you do not like anything about me... remember that I love you... wherever I am...." Dhrupad, too, had held her close, thanking his stars for she was his lifetime companion.

But who knew that her adoring words would be tested, her persona would start to change, and Dhrupad would have to travel to the unknown realms?

Soon after marriage, Dhrupad had understood that his wife had a terribly forgetful nature, so much so that this could turn into a risk to her and her surroundings.

He recalled that day morning, Ravina was in the kitchen; she was cooking their breakfast. Soon she had gone out of the kitchen to attend to a mobile phone call. Dhrupad was sitting at the dining table, reading the day's newspaper and waiting for his food and a cup of tea, after which he would start for his office. He was not aware that she had gone out of the kitchen.

Several minutes later, Dhrupad became alert when he sensed the pungent aroma of gas coming out of the kitchen. He called out, "Ravina, can you smell gas?"

Instead of the kitchen, her voice came in from the master bedroom.

"I am not in the kitchen. I am talking to my mother. Please see what is happening."

Apparently, she had forgotten entirely that she had been preparing breakfast and Dhrupad was waiting at the dining table.

Dhrupad rushed into the kitchen and found that although the breakfast was ready, the small pan containing milk, which she had put on the gas fire for making tea, had spilt, doused the fire, and as a result, the gas had started to escape and wafted in the adjoining rooms.

On this day, a major accident was avoided. If Dhrupad had not been at home, the flat and the whole building could have been on fire. He was angry and expressed his annoyance to such an extent that both refused to talk to each other for the next two days.

The third day was a Sunday; that morning, Dhrupad got up early and was busy making an official presentation on his laptop after preparing his own cup of tea. He was sitting at the dining table with a cup before him. Ravina had not left the bed; she had been sulking and had refused to start the day.

As he tentatively sipped the tea, he noticed it had gone cold. Instead of going back to the kitchen to reheat it, he went to the second bedroom to take out an official file from his briefcase. He wanted to finish his presentation first.

Returning to the table, he kept the file on it and picked up the teacup to take it to the kitchen. To his surprise, he found that the tea was piping hot. Then he observed that Ravina was in the kitchen. It was clear that during his short absence, she had got out of bed, and the first thing she did was reheat his tea. He felt pleased about her peace gesture.

On another day, midweek, Dhrupad remembered, he was in his office conference room giving his presentation when he got a call from Ravina on his mobile phone. It was from the home landline. Knowing very well that he would be busy throughout the day and not be disturbed, she should not have called him unless the need was critical.

Nevertheless, he picked up the call. Even after holding on for more than a minute, there was no response, so he called her back on her mobile phone. She did not pick up the call. He tried the landline telephone, but there was no answer. Ultimately, he managed to contact her after considerable effort through Mrs Dhamija. Then Ravina's vague response was, "Did I call you? Why? I honestly do not remember much. And am I supposed to take your calls on my mobile phone?"

And on inquiring about her not attending the landline telephone, she admitted that she had disconnected the cable; she could not give any sensible reason.

Subsequently, what struck him very odd was her comment that she had heard some voice commanding her to disconnect and not respond to his calls.

After two days, another incident shook up Dhrupad considerably. It was an early Saturday morning, a holiday, and he was still in bed when Ravina went out shopping for vegetables. She had told him about this shopping plan the previous night and that she would be back in time to prepare breakfast. She would even wake him up. By the time he woke up, it was close to 10.15 a.m., and there was no sign of his wife. He searched and, not finding her, gave her a call on her mobile phone. Unfortunately, she had forgotten to take it with her. Ultimately, he went to the main door to go out. Only it was padlocked from the outside. The result was that he could not even request any neighbour to open the door.

When Ravina returned an hour later, she had only said, "Oh my God! I had gone to the beauty parlour, which was open early. I had no plans to buy vegetables, Dhrupad; it is not my job." Naturally, Dhrupad was annoyed, but he restrained himself.

These types of weird behaviour persisted.

Then, Dhrupad reminisced about that evening when Ravina, reclining on the bed in the master bedroom, was trying to write a letter to her friend, Sudha Solanki, in the U.K. She preferred to write letters instead of sending emails. He noticed that many crumbled paper balls were casually thrown around the room; apparently, she could not complete her letter and was trying to do so. In the end, she just threw up her hand and quit. He had occasionally seen her fail to do simple tasks.

By and by, Dhrupad was becoming very anxious about her. He wanted to help her, only unhappily; she avoided him and spoke in monotones on many instances. Her face on those days became mask-like, showing no emotions.

That Monday evening, Dhrupad took Ravina to Dr Vilas Adnani. His chamber was in the main market area, not too far from his flat.

Hearing the incidents of the past two months, Dr Vilas motioned Dhrupad to come outside his chamber and told him, "Dhrupad, I am of the opinion that your wife is suffering from a mental disease called schizophrenia. Her symptoms are suggestive. She will need urgent treatment. But I must warn you that you have to be careful as she may also have homicidal tendencies, although I am not certain. In any case, I will prescribe some medicines that have to be taken regularly. Also, psychotherapy and coordinated speciality care services are needed. Please keep a strict watch on her."

Dhrupad was thunderstruck. His wife was suffering from such a disease; he had vague ideas, making him miserable. More so as he could not tell Ravina precisely what her problem was. But he could keep loving her profusely, try to make her happy, and take all the medical measures.

At the time, Ravina asked only one question, "Am I losing my mind? Will you continue to love me?"

He held her tight, showering her with kisses; she understood and sighed with happiness.

Unfortunately, that tragedy happened the following day, throwing Dhrupad's life into mayhem.

He was not feeling well and was returning early from the office. It was just after 3.35 p.m. in the afternoon. As he entered the flat, he found that Ravina had a curious expression on her face; she was perspiring profusely, her hands were shaking, and her hair and clothes were dishevelled. Abruptly she spoke in a high-pitched voice, "Dhrupad... I cannot let you do this to me... you are trying to poison me... I am a burden on you... all of you are conspiring to kill me... just now; my dead father has also warned me!"

She kept going on and on. He attempted to appease her, but she could not be held back. In the end, getting out of the flat, she went to Mrs Dhamija's flat and started repeating the same allegations. With great difficulty, she could be pacified. Dhrupad understood that she was hallucinating and showed signs of delirium, typical of schizophrenia.

In the evening, after an early dinner, as soon as Dhrupad had gone to the master bedroom and was waiting for her to join him on the bed when he heard a shriek. Ravina was screaming in the second bedroom. Getting up in haste, he rushed to her, and as he stepped inside the bedroom, he saw that she was on the balcony, and before his disbelieving eyes, before he could do anything, she climbed over the railings and jumped down. Her cry spread into the gloom of the night and became feeble as she hurtled down towards the ground, ten floors below; then, a sound followed by an abrupt silence.

Ravina had taken her own life!

What happened next was a series of unrelenting tribulations for Dhrupad. Soon the ambulance arrived, and Ravina was taken to the nearby City hospital, but she was already dead by that time. The police too reached, and Dhrupad was taken to the station for questioning.

In the days that followed, he, unfortunately, realised that, as her husband, he was the prime suspect in her unnatural death. That it was a mere suicide and not abetment to suicide or a murder committed by him became the issue with the police; more so, as Ravina had revealed to Mrs Dhamija on the day of her death that she doubted that her husband was attempting to poison her.

Soon the police started behaving very irrationally with him, were deeply suspicious about his motives, and it seemed that they would seek his prosecution for the death of his wife. They were unconvinced of her schizophrenic inclinations even after consulting the doctor. These were unthinkable to him! He knew he was innocent, deeply loved her, and his conviction would be the most severe tragedy of his life!

As Dhrupad sat alone in his locked flat that Friday night, stimulating his memories, he suddenly realised with a shudder that the supernatural incidents of the last few hours had a deep meaning. The blank calls on his mobile phone, disconnection of landline telephone, switching off of the gas, unexpected heating of tea, locking up of the main door, et al. were all intricately linked to similar types of past incidents which had originated out of Ravina's behaviour under the influence of schizophrenia!

Ravina was everywhere, everything! Not only that, but he could even smell his favourite fragrance of Ravina.

What exactly did that mean, anyway? Was her soul now in the flat and trying to tell him something? But what and why?

What was more, he strongly felt that he was missing some other link or clue which he could not fathom!

Perhaps something existing here would solve this bizarre mystery.

Getting up, he decided that he should search every nook and corner of the flat. He then went into the master bedroom. This was where she used to keep her personal things and spent most of her time and hence needed to be examined first.

Looking around, checking behind the curtains, inside her wooden almirah, the dressing table, the double bed, and other furniture, he could not find anything which could give rise to any clue. He then went to the attached bathroom and returned to the bedroom, not being any wiser. As a last resort, he bent down to examine below the bed, and then he noticed numerous crumbled paper balls lying under it, virtually out of sight in a corner. It was somewhat unusual since the rooms were swept every day, but apparently, the maid overlooked them.

Was the missing link here? Picking up each of the paper balls and smoothening them out, he found that these were from her writing pad. Many of those crumbled papers were blank, some had a few lines of half-written letters, and as he checked the last one, suddenly he became alert.

It was really brief, and her handwriting was unmistakable. As he narrowed his eyes to read it with some difficulty, his breath stopped for a moment. The words were revealing:

'*I am sick. I cannot live like this. This is horrible. Nobody is responsible for my death. Dhrupad will understand. Love him.*'

As Dhrupad read this, he realised with a jolt that it was a suicide note from Ravina; with this, he could be free of all accusations of causing her death!

He would now prove his innocence to the police, particularly that obnoxious Inspector Pyarelal Choubey!

The police initially did not find this by some weird coincidence when they had thoroughly searched this room after her death. Was it written by Ravina before or after her death?

No matter what, her love percolating through her diseased mind and from the spectral world was always with him.

CHAPTER THREE

WAS SHE REAL?

That day was in April, and I clearly recalled that I was with Bini in the coffee shop adjacent to our college. The coffee in our cups was untouched, getting cold, but we were happily oblivious of that. I was looking at her eyes, unblinking and her gaze was on me; I was also holding her soft hand. During that misty pink haze, Tina came in; I had not noticed her. Putting her bag on the table with some force, Tina cleared her throat and said somewhat loudly, "Excuse me, can I just interfere?" Did I detect a touch of annoyance in her voice? She would be, I thought, as she fancied herself to be my long-term girlfriend.

I hastily removed my hand from Bini's and turned towards Tina with a smile on my face, although I felt irritated at this sudden intrusion. When Tina left, somehow pacified, I apologised to Bini.

I wanted them both; it was fun!

The next day at the college, we were introduced to a new young lady who had joined another class section. It was the beginning of a new academic session. Before I could ask her name, I became mesmerised by her appearance. She was taller than me, somewhat plump with a husky, sexy voice, but that was unimportant. The most striking feature was her complexion; I did not seem to remember seeing such unblemished fairness. That her name was Kuhu Rohatgi registered a little later. By then, I had decided to definitely introduce myself properly after the classes. She seemed to be a person with whom I could have a nice fling. More joy!

That evening, I talked to a group of my friends and showed off. I was pleased since, during the day, I had befriended Kuhu, and she had agreed to have dinner and go to a movie with me during the weekend. Another one of my achievements!

And that was not the end. For the next several weeks, I met Kuhu regularly, and I enjoyed myself thoroughly interacting with a kind and decent persona. However, the only catch was that she took this relationship far too seriously; in fact, once she had said she would die if she could not get me, perhaps my reputation would have reached her ears. However, such emotions did not impress me; I always wanted to be a free bird.

Moving away from my so-called romantic journey with Kuhu, I would now dwell upon my accomplishments because the ladies fell for me. I was a brilliant student in college, a successful footballer representing my institution for the past two seasons, a sought-after rock–singer, and a ruggedly handsome tall young man, if I might modestly say so. But perhaps my image as a Casanova preceded all other qualities.

My life was happily sailing with those backdrops, but soon I had a disconcerting experience that changed my existence.

It was the morning of another Monday, a couple of months later, when I came out of the botany class after it was over and started walking through the long corridor of the college building.

Walking towards me from a distance in that passageway, I saw another new young lady with her black hair tied severely in a bun and dark-rimmed glasses. She was slim and had an average complexion and height. As she came near, it was apparent that her face was exceedingly pretty with classic features of large, beautiful eyes, aquiline nose, and curved lips.

Although I have had many affairs in the past, this young lady stirred emotions in me as nobody had till now. And this had happened only in a few minutes; unbelievable! I just stared as she turned left into another room. I was unsure whether she noticed me among the many students in the corridor, but I was convinced that I would get to know her soon.

That chance came sooner than expected as we happened to get introduced to each other through a common friend in the college canteen the same day.

Her name was Garima Bose.

She was different from other ladies whom I knew in college. Painfully shy and given to few words, she was an enigma to me. I was not used to that. Being gregarious, I always sought female and male friends to match my attitude. But then, this utterly different nature of Garima seemed to attract me immensely.

The problem was, could I reveal that feeling so early in our acquaintance, although I had the reputation to do just that?

Meanwhile, Kuhu had left the college and shifted to Mumbai since her father took a transfer from the Delhi office to that City.

That Thursday, about a month later, during which period I met Garima occasionally, more out of chance than by any design, she came into my classroom, which was empty. I was sitting there trying to understand a particularly complex piece of biological hypothesis; my thought process had to proceed unhindered.

Garima walked towards the desk where I was sitting, and I looked up at her with surprise; her visit was the last thing I had expected.

She said, "Sorry to bother you, Vaasu, but I need your help in my studies. Is it possible?"

Looking at her, I could make out that she was earnest. Knowing her nature, it was also apparent that she seriously needed help. Suddenly I felt a faint palpitation of my heart, and my mouth turned dry in some nervousness. It was peculiar; I was not a person to be afflicted by such reactions, at least not on seeing any woman. But this lady was different.

"Yes, what do you want...?" I managed to say.

She had some doubts about the chapter on cross-pollination in botany, which we discussed. I could say with some pride that my understanding of the subject was exemplary; many of my friends did take my help regularly, so it was not difficult to clarify her questions.

About an hour later, we were through and gathering our books and notes we came out of the empty class.

"How about a cup of coffee in the canteen?" I asked. She hesitated for a second before agreeing; I was sure that my help, a little while ago, must have had a salutary effect on her mind.

I settled down comfortably after bringing two cups of cappuccino from the canteen- kitchen and placing them on the table. There was no immediate chore to attend to, and her company made me feel good. It was anybody's guess how she was feeling about me, if at all.

We were sipping coffee and discussing more botany when she suddenly asked, "Are you planning to marry soon after the final exams?" She was looking at me intently; her eyes without eyeliners were partly hidden behind her glasses, but their hypnotic effect was not lost on me. Taken aback a bit, I recovered and said with a chuckle, "Most of us will marry sometime..."

I did not want to give any direct reply.

She leaned forward, her lips curled with a hint of a smile, "Who will be the lucky woman? Tina, Bini, or Kuhu? Or is there any other about whom I do not know yet?"

I managed to blush; my face must have had shown my embarrassment; looking sideways at her; I said, "It seems that my reputation as a womaniser is playing on your mind."

Now it was her turn to be abashed. "No... no... that is not what I meant."

We changed the topic, but I realised that the subject was playing in her mind. Why? Did she have any interest in my affairs with other young ladies? What was her true feeling? It was tough to understand women and their thoughts, but I was sure that she would not have any inkling about my true attraction for her. Or was I wrong?

Some months later, we were toiling with our final examinations. My preparations were average, but I did not bother; my attempt was up to my standards anyway. If the results were in the same lines as my earlier ones, I should be topping the chart. But there was always a slip between the cup and the lip. In any case, I would know the result a month later. Meanwhile, I would have to plan for my further studies.

In the interim, it was relaxation time.

That evening I had a gala time with my friends in the most happening restaurant in the town. With food and drinks in abundance and everybody letting their hair down, the time passed in a jiffy. There was only one hitch in my happiness; Garima was the only absentee at the party.

The following day on a Sunday, I called her at about 9.00 a.m., "Why did not you come to the party last evening? We … rather I particularly missed you." She remained silent for a few moments, then said, "Sorry, I was not well… had a severe headache and cold."

I pondered a bit, "Hope you are better now," then, slightly pausing, asked, "can we meet for lunch at the 'Food joint' restaurant today at 12.30 p.m.?" She remained quiet for so long that I thought she had not heard me, then, with an almost inaudible voice, said, "I am not sure, will let you know."

Then, unfortunately, at around 11.30 a.m. I accidentally dropped and broke my mobile phone. While I was contemplating calling her around 11:45 a.m. from my landline phone, as she did not know that number, I got a call from her at that time itself on my landline. I guessed that somebody had given that number to her earlier.

In any case, Garima's voice was more assured and precise this time. "Vaasu, instead of going to a restaurant, can you not come to my house today for dinner? My mother has gone out of town, but I am sure I can make something palatable for you to eat." Her voice sounded husky, and I was sure it was due to her cold and cough.

At any rate, it was delightfully unexpected, and I agreed. She then gave me the direction to reach her house.

It was late evening when I arrived at her house.

Before that, I had to go to the shop to give my mobile phone for repairs.

Garima opened the door and stepped aside. As my eyes rested on her, I stared. Her appearance had undergone a metamorphosis. Sans her glasses, eyeliner enhancing her gorgeous eyes, a touch of pink on her shapely lips, open silky hair up to her shoulders, wearing a light pink sari and matching blouse, she looked dazzling, and she knew it.

A sweet fragrance enveloped her, which was unusual since I had never seen her wear perfume. It accentuated her beauty, but the scent seemed to be very familiar. I then recalled that Kuhu used this perfume often. But what did it matter? What Garima wore now was more important to me.

With a smile, Garima escorted me into her drawing-room

Looking around, I said appreciatively, "You have a nice drawing-room, Garima."

She nodded, made me comfortable on a huge sofa, and went inside the kitchen to get me something to drink.

Keeping the glass of cold beer on the table, she sat down on the other end of the sofa where I was sitting.

I said, "Well, your invitation is totally out of the blue, and if I may say so, you look so beautiful... I have never seen you like this before."

She looked down at her hands and silently acknowledged with a suggestion of a smile. "It was so good of you to have come." There was a hint of tears in her eyes. "This is the only way I could get you alone."

I glanced around, "I know your mother is not in; I do not see anybody else."

"Tonight, there is no one but me... I am your only hostess."

Again, that feeling of nervousness was returning to me; this lady was really different in my eyes. I had to admit that she was so special, and why not? She was my first real love!

Seeing me quiet and thinking, she said, "Everything OK, Vaasu?"

"Yes ... yes." I took hold of my emotions and tried to start a topic. I wanted to know her plans after the declaration of college results. We discussed the pros and cons of various future career options. Almost half an hour had elapsed when she said, "I will serve your dinner."

As she was about to get up, abruptly, the entire house plunged into darkness. The streetlights too shut down. There was a load shedding in that locality; usually, this happened during the summer season.

In the darkness, her voice was audible. "I will search for the candles. Our standby supply has gone bad; I will need some light. My mobile is on the side table next to you. Will you pick it up and switch on the torch?" She gave me the password to unlock her mobile.

Here a passing thought struck me. Why has the standby electricity supply in her house gone bad? I knew she was very particular about her household affairs. Well, whatever did it matter?

Picking up her mobile phone, I switched on its light and stood up to guide her. She, too, got up and moved inside the house; I followed her to illuminate the way. She walked into her kitchen, opened several drawers, searched, and finally took out a candle and a matchbox. I stood near her.

While I was waiting, watching her, my heartbeat accelerated. Her closeness, absence of any other person in the house, and the darkness invited me to touch her, take her in my arms, and kiss her. But no! I might be a womaniser; I would not touch or take any advantage of this lady. She was much too vulnerable; I would always protect her. Did I not love her?

At this time, fleetingly, the thought about Kuhu came to me; she said some time ago that she also loved me, but I did not reciprocate. What I was doing right now, was it correct? I pushed that idea aside.

Garima turned and walked into the drawing-room; I followed her back.

After lighting the candle, we sat down on the sofa again. She was a little nearer than last time. Her face had a soft look which I could make out even in the light and shade of the candle. Her eyes were on me... were they saying something?

I wiped the sweat on my face, picked up the beer glass, and sipped it. She said, "Can I offer you another glass, something else?" I shook my head.

We chatted about various subjects; surprisingly, we had many common interests and views. But my predominant thought was on her; was it the right time to tell her that I loved her?

The power supply came almost an hour later when we were together.

She again got up to serve dinner when I offered to help. We walked into the kitchen, and as my hand brushed against her, she stopped and looked at me.

Then, miraculously, she took hold of my right hand. I could feel her soft and yielding palm, ice-cold, and she pulled me near her; so near that her body was touching mine, her face was near me; she then felt her lips with mine. It was cold as well. Her kiss sent a shiver through me as if it was my first experience. My eyes closed automatically in sheer pleasure, and then I got another peculiar sensation as if she were taller than me and chubby like Kuhu, but I ignored that.

"I love you...!" She whispered.

I did not know why, but my voice choked. "But why do you love me? I am a Casanova... I am a womanizer... I have a bad reputation among ladies at the college." I could say no more.

She again kissed me, a reassuring one, and said, "I do not care what you are, but I know you are right for me. You are the real man and mine. Or else you would have taken advantage of me in this secluded house, forced upon me sexually in the darkness, but you did not. Tonight, I only took the initiative to make you come near me."

She then held my face looking intently, "You love me, right? I know you love me!"

This was eternal happiness! And I was truthful for the first time with a lady, "Garima... I love you too... I am crazy about you!"

The dinner which followed was sumptuous.

Later, we were back on the sofa and relaxing when I thought it was the best time to clear my small doubts. I said, "Was the standby electricity supply of the house really not working when there was load shedding?"

She hesitated, shaking her head, "No, I had switched it off intentionally! To see if you misuse the position of this darkness and try to misbehave with me; of course, you did not, like I said."

I understood that she had assessed my intentions, and why not? I was a lady-killer, but I seemed to have passed my most challenging examination, that of her love and faith.

There was one other question that was on my lips. "How come your body is so cold?" I asked.

"I am not well; did I not tell you?"

I was satisfied with her reply.

It was late in the night, past 1.30 a.m., and I wanted to leave, although my mind was not up to it. It was a natural human emotion to remain with your loved person as long as possible, especially when the relationship had just begun to flourish.

Garima felt; likewise, I was sure and requested me to stay on for the night. As we sat on the sofa and talked for hours, the time seemed to slip by effortlessly when at last, she appeared sleepy. And that made me sleepy too, and we held each other's hands while embarking on a dream world in her bedroom.

It was early Monday morning when my eyes opened, and I found that Garima was not with me. I got up and called out, "Garima, where are you? I think I should leave now, meet you at the college."

There was no reply, but I could hear the shower in the washroom. Without wanting to bother her, I left her house.

This could have been the end of a perfect love story, but fate had other plans for me!

A couple of hours later, I started for my college. I wanted to pick up my mobile phone from the shop, but it was not ready. I could pick it up in the evening.

When I entered my classroom about fifteen minutes before the scheduled time, my mind was joyful, and the weather seemed to be resonating with my mood with a sunny, cloudless blue sky, chirping birds, and a mild and cool breeze percolating through the four large windows of the room. I immediately thought of giving the good news to my group of close friends sitting scattered in various seats. In fact, I was also planning to have a small get-together after college hours, in the canteen. Winning Garima's love was definitely a cause for celebration.

I noticed that Garima had not yet come.

But what I encountered there was totally unexpected.

Rahul, Shashank, Saloni, and Rattan were sitting together at one corner of the room, talking in a low tone with seriousness writ large on their faces, and Priya and Selva were seated a little apart, huddled together and observing me with apparent tears in their eyes.

What was going on?

I walked up to Selva and Priya and looked around my friends.

"What have we here? Why you guys are so serious?" My voice sounded a bit shaky.

Shaloni came to me and touched my arm, "Don't you know, Vaasu?"

"What?"

"Garima met with an accident today morning ... while driving to the college! She is no more!"

Immediately my senses reeled; it was as if I was hit by a bolt of lightning, my legs became weak, and my head started throbbing!

The whole incident of last evening and night flashed in my mind, slowly and painfully, as though that was a dream which was now turning into a nightmare.

What a tragedy that happened after I left her in the morning!

By that time, I had slumped on a chair, and my friends and others in the classroom converged on me with reactions of solace. They all knew my feelings for Garima.

That day I could not attend my classes and returned home. My friends promised to come after college hours.

Sitting alone in my room in the afternoon, I held my head in my hands, and my eyes refused to remain dry; this was a shock of my lifetime; I did not know how long my life would remain.

Yes, I realised in this tragedy that my life would be nothing without Garima!

It was an eternity when I managed to control my senses and then got up; I would call her mother; I needed to be at her side during grief. Priya had given her number. I used my landline to call her, as my mobile phone was still in repair.

When she took my call, her voice was breaking. "Vaasu, why is God so unkind to me?" She sobbed. "Last year, I lost my husband, and today I have lost my only daughter. I had asked her not to go to the college since we were out of town, and she had to do a lot of self-driving from there on the highway, which she was not used to, but she never listened to me... now this!"

While I was listening to her, suddenly, my sixth sense started flashing! What did she say? Was Garima out of town last night and not at her residence? Then how come I met her last evening and was with her throughout the previous night? This was downright odd!

By that time, she had disconnected.

I called her mother again. "Aunty, was anybody at your residence last night? Just wanted to check."

"No, beta, the house was locked. She was not there; if she were, her routine drive to her college at a short distance would not have been fatal! She would not have died on the highway. Destiny, my child, destiny!"

I slowly kept the phone headset on the cradle and started thinking. Nothing was making any sense. Who was the young woman I met yesterday evening and spent the whole night at Garima's home? Not her?

All of a sudden, I shivered; a cold, clammy fear seemed to clutch at my psyche. With a visible effort, I had to come out of this feeling.

In the evening, I collected my repaired mobile phone. Many missed calls were there, one of which was received yesterday at 12.00 noon from Garima. And then there was a message from her soon after. She had written that she could neither contact my mobile phone, nor could she talk to me as she did not know my any other number, so she was constrained to send this message. She regretted that our lunch at 12.30 p.m. yesterday would not happen as she was going out of town, unexpectedly, to her mother for some urgent work.

Now, the most bizarre part!

My mobile phone was already broken at 11.30 a.m. yesterday, and weirdly someone, sounding like Garima but with a husky voice, had called me on my landline at around 11.45 a.m. although I thought Garima was not aware of that number, someone had given her earlier. But that was not so, as was clear from her message subsequently.

So, who called me and fixed the evening dinner?

I did not have to wait for long!

Two days later, during which time I was in a miserable mood, Priya called me as I was about to go to bed.

"Another bad news, Vaasu. Do you remember Kuhu Rohatgi, that woman you flirted with and who had fallen so much head over heels over you in love that she said she would die if she did not get you? She had shifted to Mumbai earlier."

I nodded; I always remembered her. Now what?

"Well," she continued, "Kuhu is dead; she committed suicide a couple of months ago in that City. And the revealing part is that in her suicide note, she said that you were the reason for her sadness and death ...."

Oh my God!

Priya went on, but my mind was now in a tizzy. Was this the answer to the mystery of that evening and the night? Was that young lady who was with me not Garima but Kuhu, disguised as Garima, in a mystical body?

I now recall that Kuhu was aware of my landline number. And then, the doubts about those subtle and intuitive hints about Garima's height, plumpness, and perfume, indicating that the woman physically close to me was not Garima but Kuhu became clear!

So, did Kuhu's ghost make love to me in the guise of Garima inside her own house even when Garima was alive and with her mother in the neighbouring town? Perhaps Kuhu's passion made her do all these!

And was Kuhu responsible for Garima's accidental death? I had my doubts; she was thoroughly a nice person with no malice! But did her passion reach the limit of madness?

In the end, my love failed, and would I honestly blame myself for my nature as a 'ladies' man for this? Who would know?

Many questions remained unanswered!

I could only imagine that I had lived through a paranormal event that I never believed in!

CHAPTER FOUR

SHADOWY MALE

Laboni Sarkar shut down her computer on her work desk, got up, hung her purse on her shoulders, picked up the briefcase and mobile phone, and walked out of her office after digitally signing off. The time was 7.17 p.m.

This late Saturday winter evening in Meerut's suburban office complex, she found that she was the last to leave her office. That was not unusual as her duties generally made her stay late on almost all working days; another reason was that her residential flat was located not too far away, requiring about thirty-five minutes' walk to reach; so she could afford to stay those extra hours. She also preferred to stay in shape as she walked at every opportunity.

As she stepped out of the office building onto the main road and turned left, she found that some of the streetlights at a distance were not working, thus throwing patches of lights and shadows on the road winding ahead.

The area opposite the office building, covering the other side of the road, was expansive and empty till eyes could fathom, with some half-constructed buildings barely visible afar due to the sporadic lit bulbs in those places.

Her office was situated at the end of a row of buildings on the right-back, and so she had to walk about a kilometer on the road towards the left side to reach the subsequent chain of buildings. The intermediate area had no office with an enormous public park with bushes, flowers, large trees, and well-manicured lawns.

This evening, aggravating the partial darkness, the roads were utterly deserted since all the offices in this area had closed a long time ago, and the people had gone home.

In any case, all these neither posed any problems for her nor was she scared of any known or unknown dangers, which she thought were very unlikely.

She knew that Vikram Kar, her fiancé, would disagree with her risk-taking attitude, but that was who she was.

Apart from being courageous, Laboni was a pretty woman in a conventional sense. She was without any makeup, had long black hair tied tightly in a bun, wore black-rimmed glasses that partially hid her lotus-shaped eyes, and had a petite nose and shapely pale pink lips. Her slim figure was attired in a simple cotton blue saree with a woollen shawl thrown over her shoulders. After glancing at the wristwatch strapped to her right wrist, she walked briskly; black utility sandals encased her feet.

Since this walk was a routine, always uneventful, her mind was more preoccupied with the work she had to plan for the next week than about her security or any other danger.

However, she had an unexpected experience that evening.

While walking briskly, when her attention was more on her mobile phone, she perceived something was amiss. This was the first time she sensed danger, and it was an uncomfortable feeling. Semi darkness prevailed in the area, as one of the adjacent streetlights did not function, and she was about halfway along the length of the public park to the left.

Stopping for a moment, she looked towards the deserted park with low railings, which had decorative mid-height lit lamps scattered inside; then, not finding anything suspicious, she glanced at the other side of the road. Apart from the open space and the dimly lit constructions at a distance, she could not see anything else. She then glanced back sharply but could only see the deserted road. Not being any wiser, she shook her head slightly and resumed walking, albeit faster, although she was not seriously worried.

Moments later, she again felt the same danger, and now without stopping but slowing down, she squinted at the park and suddenly realised that she could have momentarily seen a shadow of a person moving behind a tree and heard a rustling noise. Were her eyes and ears playing tricks on her? She stopped and watched intently. The fact was that nothing else was visible or heard; she did not think it fit to stand and walked away rapidly, reaching the following chain of buildings on the left where she could see human activities.

Subsequently, she reached her flat without any incident or uncomfortable feelings.

Not giving importance to the incident, Laboni did her usual activities the next day, and by Monday, she was in the office wholly immersed in work. During the early evening, when the office work was over, she thought for a few seconds about Saturday night's unpleasant experience before coming out but soon pushed it out of her mind for more urgent matters. With her two colleagues who accompanied her at that time, and the road not being deserted with sufficient traffic, her trip was absolutely uneventful.

Almost a month had passed when she was returning home from the office that day, and by that time, Laboni had forgotten entirely about the earlier experience. An important meeting had just concluded, and the office closed late. The time was almost 9.00 p.m., and after refusing an offer to give her a lift to her home by her seniors, she was walking on the same road as she had been doing for the last many months. The winter fog was setting in, and the atmosphere was tranquil, broken only by the sound of a few vehicles; even the gentle noise of insects like katydids, crickets, and cicadas could be heard from inside the park.

When she reached the same halfway spot near the park on her left side, she distinctly heard a different noise emanating from behind a large tree. It sounded like somebody was calling her by name! That night all the streetlights illuminated the area well enough to enable her to see that a man was definitely standing there, hidden. She thought that she should face this problem squarely.

"Who is there?" She called in a loud voice. A few pedestrians walking nearby paused to glance at her.

There was no reply, but Laboni had decided to check this and swiftly walked towards the side gate of the park next to the tree; then, she heard the footsteps of somebody running away.

And when she saw the man who had turned his head fleetingly to see her, she was shaken to the core!

What kind of nightmare was that? Was this man, Umang Sinha, her former lover? His face with a beard and more so his long curly hair, faintly visible even from that distance, seemed to suggest that!

How could that be? He was her past, her admirer during her days in the City college in the adjoining town of Sonipat; it was the period of third-year commerce graduation! How many years had passed since then? She tried to remember; at least seven years had gone by.

Umang, a brilliant student, had fallen head over heels for her during those days, and they did have a little more than a year of togetherness. He had a certain charisma, and perhaps the relationship could have blossomed, but tragedy struck when, one day, she realised that he was also a so-called *Casanova*, trying to woo some of her close friends – Juhi, Rachna, to name a few. It made Laboni furious and upset. She was always an intense girl by temperament and took her relationship quite seriously. This unfaithfulness of Umang was totally unacceptable. Soon she parted ways with him, and by that time, she had completed her graduation and moved to another college to complete her MBA. After that, there was no communication of any type with him, and he seemed to have evaporated from her memory over the years. Or was that the case?

But now, so many years later, she had come across Umang! And that too in such a weird circumstance. Why was he acting like a stalker? Why did he run away when they knew each other so well? The entire incident of today made no sense at all. And what about the earlier episode? That meant he was repeatedly following her over time and perhaps intended to do that in the future. What was his intention? Was it to win her back?

She knew Umang very well and felt that he could never behave in such a way even with all his faults. In the end, she became almost sanguine that the man was not Umang, but her mind was still vacillating. Who called her?

All these thoughts had made her stay rooted to where she was standing for some minutes. Then, as she turned away, she thought she heard a rustling noise! Had Umang come back? Stopping, she tilted her head towards the sound to listen better, but was no wiser and slightly shaking her head, she started walking; she had enough for that night.

After that nocturnal encounter, Laboni became wary of this kind of harassment. Whoever that stalker was, she seriously thought she should complain to the police. The local SHO, Ramveer Yash, was known to her; however, she would not disclose her doubts about Umang.

When she finally met the SHO two days later, he was willing to help but had his limitations.

"Madam, this type of problem is becoming serious in our City; I have received many complaints from women from various walks of life, but I can only advise you to take precautions with our limited patrolling resources."

That night after retiring to bed, she could not sleep. Her thoughts were continually on Umang. Should she check about him from their common friend, Dimpi Sarathi?

The following day when she called Dimpi, the friend was unsure.

"Umang is neither in Sonipat nor in this City, that I can say." She replied.

"Where has he gone? Any idea?" Laboni asked.

"Don't think so."

"At least do you know what he does nowadays?"

After these years, Laboni was suddenly curious to know.

"Nothing much, I believe. After completing his degree course, he somehow became a waster... had no ambition, no perseverance, nothing positive ... did some jobs in the IT sector but did not persist."

"I see. Any reason?"

There was a pause at the other end. Then Dimpi said, "You should know better… not getting your love was what broke him completely."

"What are you saying? He loved so many females. This could be due to any one of them." Laboni responded in a faint voice; her voice seemed stifled.

"I'm not so sure," Dimpi said.

After the conversation, Laboni felt troubled. Deep down, she realised that Umang meant more to her than she wanted to admit to herself these years!

It was lunchtime at the office when Laboni got a call on her mobile phone.

"Madam, SHO, Ramveer Yash, speaking. The other day you came to me about your problem. Madam, I thought I should warn you that a man had been spotted near your office area stalking a few women these months. I received complaints from them. This man has been described as having a short height with a mass of unruly hair and beard. According to our sources, he is a psychopath stalking women for sex crimes. Till now, he has been unsuccessful. We think we can identify him. Anyway, we will trace and arrest him, but in the meanwhile, please do take care."

When Laboni came out of her office after lunch for her usual stroll, her mind was in turmoil. Her sixth sense was telling her that the psychopath was Umang. He had been tracking her and other women; his womanising habits of earlier years had not diminished; in fact, he had become a criminal now!

She felt more depressed because she did not expect a man as competent as Umang to throw away his everyday life just because of his failed love life.

Her thoughts now meandered. Was she his real love? And did she actually love him and unfairly reject him only due to his immature Casanova nature? Who knew, had she accepted him, he would have been a normal human being. Somehow, she felt responsible for all these tragedies. But can she do anything now to rescue Umang from his present condition and usher him into a new life?

During the night, Laboni called Dimpi again.

"Do you have a mobile phone number of Umang? I want to contact him." She said.

"No, I do not have; sorry! Any particular reason?"

Unwilling to reveal her tortured thought process about her former lover, she diverted the subject. As she disconnected, Laboni wondered how to contact him, which seemed difficult.

The next evening after the office, Laboni was walking down the main stairs to reach the road when she saw him.

Umang was waiting for her near the lamppost.

He looked the same as she remembered him during her college days. Of course, she had also seen him that night in the park, running away, but only a glimpse.

His familiar slim build, short height, boyish face, and a mass of curly hair and beard with the casual dress of jeans and t-shirt brought a touch of nostalgia. These years had not touched his countenance.

"Hello Laboni, long time no see!" Even his smile was predictable. When he approached her, his mild body odour, which she remembered over the years, still enveloped him.

Laboni's body seemed weak at that time, but she tried to cope with her initial reaction by holding on to her briefcase and mobile phone a little more firmly; thence, she smiled back at him.

"Hello! Never expected to see you so suddenly...!" Her voice shook a bit.

"I knew you wanted my mobile phone number from Dimpi, but then I thought it best to meet you personally. I could not dare to do this earlier since last time you had warned me not to meet you, ever."

With a wave of her hand, Laboni said, "Forget about the past; come to the coffee shop and let us talk."

Walking side by side to the corner coffee shop, Laboni recalled with a touch of emotion those years when they used to visit coffee shops so often, hand in hand!

Today, of course, they maintained a discreet distance.

After ordering coffee, she thoughtfully looked at him sitting across the tiny table. How would she start?

"Umang, so many years have passed, but I have always remembered you...." These words came spontaneously from her heart. Inwardly she winced; she could have been more circumspect.

He was watching her closely and then spoke in a low tone. "I forever loved you, wanted to be with you, to meet you, these years, only you did not wish and allow me...." He looked down to hide the moistness in his eyes and conceal his real feelings.

Laboni understood all his sentiments, her emotions were in resonance, but this was not the time to reciprocate. Life had gone ahead too far, and she could not return to her college days. Her marriage to Vikram, her fiancé, was imminent. Today's mission was, of course, different, to help him into a new life.

Taking a sip from the coffee cup, she chose her words carefully.

"You been following me! You called my name that night inside the park. Why?"

Umang seemed embarrassed. He said, "I have told you; I craved to meet you but could not come near you earlier because you stopped that! What else could I do?"

"This is not the way! Like a stalker! My God! And I was told you were trailing other women, too, with criminal intentions. Have you not given up your womanising habits of college years?" She sounded annoyed.

"Who told you that?"

"The police."

He shook his head.

"They are absolutely wrong. I only followed you! And that too to save you from danger and to take care. I am not a criminal; believe me, Laboni! I am the sufferer, the victim, and I want justice!" There was a sincere plea in his voice.

Laboni kept quiet for some time. This was somewhat unexpected, but she somehow believed him. It was the police's job to apprehend the real stalker; who was she to suspect an innocent man?

"Anyway, please do not follow me henceforth; if you want to meet me any time, we can do so as friends... as good friends."

As Umang kept quiet, Laboni said, "And please return to your normal life, follow a career, and I am always with you to support you."

That day, she and Umang spoke for a long time. In the end, she felt that she could instil positivity and a new purpose in his life.

While leaving him, she shook hands with him.

"Why is your hand so cold and clammy?" She asked.

"I am slightly indisposed, but I will be alright very soon."

More than two weeks had passed since then, Umang had not communicated with her, and she could not contact him since he did not have a mobile phone and had assured her that he would get in touch with her from time to time. That was acceptable to her.

She did not tell about Umang to anybody.

It was Friday night, around 8.35 p.m., and Laboni was delayed at the office due to an urgent assignment. She was carrying a load of work that she would have to complete that night itself.

Her mind was preoccupied when she reached the same spot near the public park on her left side, and after that, she distinctively heard a noise emanating from behind a large tree. Umang appeared to be standing there, partially hidden. Why was he up to his old mischief again? She entered the park to admonish him when suddenly she felt a strong arm around her neck from the rear, which almost choked her, then he turned her around forcibly to kiss her, and she saw him. There was sufficient light to see him.

And that man was not Umang!

At that shocking moment, she realised this man also had long hair and a beard, but not curly. This was the real stalker, the criminal psychopath, and unfortunately, she had now become his victim!

She tried to scream but could not as her mouth was brutally covered by his rough mouth; his hand was groping her body; she attempted to strike free but could not do so; in the struggle, both lost balance and collapsed on the hard ground.

As she hit her head when she fell and was losing consciousness, she faintly heard her attacker give a horrendous scream which faded into oblivion in her departing senses and perceived that his grip had loosened.

She did not remember anything after that!

On waking up on the hospital bed feeling groggy with intense pain in her body and head, she saw, with half-open eyes, SHO, Ramveer Yash, standing at the bedside and a nurse.

Seeing her, he bent down and said, "Madam, good to see you recovering; you have been fortunate to escape from the clutches of that criminal psychopath who could have raped you, but we cannot understand how he met his end...."

Laboni tried to concentrate; her head was throbbing; she said weakly, "What? I have no idea...."

"No problem, we will meet later after you fully recuperate, and we get the autopsy done of that dead man." The SHO said soothingly.

Ten days later, Laboni met Ramveer Yash at the police station.

He said, "Madam, your attacker has been identified. His name was Hameer Dayal, and he was a criminal. In fact, he was a fugitive after committing murder in Kanpur. The police were searching for him and suspected that he would be in this City. That he was the criminal psychopath, here, we were not too sure."

The inspector paused to take out a photo of the criminal and showed it to Laboni, who confirmed that man indeed had attacked her.

"This man's death is due to a heart seizure triggered by extreme terror. Something made him die in an excruciating manner; his face reflected the fear he must have encountered. But what or who did this? A mysterious death indeed!" The inspector shook his head in perplexity.

"In any case, thank goodness you are safe, and the public will also be from now on."

It appeared that the police would never solve this mystery.

Nonetheless, there was a revealing twist to these bewildering events.

A week later, Laboni received a call from Dimpi.

"Laboni, I have news for you; you made enquiries about Umang, well now I know the latest; sadly, he died about four months ago in Kanpur, murdered by a criminal called Hameer Dayal. His name the police had circulated to the general public recently, as he escaped and was on the run."

Dimpi did not stop speaking, but Laboni could no longer listen. Although her mind refused to believe it, she realised with a mixed feeling of deepening sorrow and trepidation followed by a shiver that she had repeatedly come across the ghost of Umang during the past two months.

However, it was gradually becoming evident to her that there were a lot of complexities in the encounters with him and more! Initially, Umang was present but not visible, near or inside that public park, when that criminal psychopath was waiting to rape and kill her. At that time, she had a weird experience but luckily remained safe. Later, Umang revealed himself in a human form to her inside the park during another night, but fleetingly! That criminal was also there; fortunately, no untoward incident happened that night too!

After that, when Umang understood that Laboni recognised him and wanted to get in touch with him, he again appeared, now in a human form, interacted with her in the coffee shop, and understood that she still had feelings for him.

Knowing this, satisfied, it seemed Umang would have gone out of her life, but there was another angle! Hameer Dayal had murdered him earlier, and he had to get justice and take revenge. He waited for that criminal psychopath for this retribution, during which he found that Hameer was, in fact, continuously stalking Laboni. This was totally unacceptable. The flashpoint came when that criminal psychopath moved in to rape and kill Laboni that night, and then there was no control. The ghost of Umang finally stepped in, the idea was to destroy Hameer by fright, so it was anybody's guess what gruesome form he had converted himself.

And the ultimate result was that Hameer Dayal died unnaturally out of sheer horror!

This brought the curtain down to the eeriest of romances, leaving Laboni emotionally shaken! Tears often shone in Laboni's eyes for Umang, her rejected lover whom she would never have or actually had but who would remain in her memories forever!

CHAPTER FIVE

SUPERNATURAL MOMENTS

Deeti Ahuja was my co-worker at the office, but she was not only that, actually much more, emotionally and otherwise. We used to exchange helpful tips on official matters during those early days; she was always supportive, even when she had no commitments or duties to perform. As the days, weeks, and years passed, I recognised how much I liked interacting with her; her intelligence and integrity captivated me. Aside from that, her attractive personality charmed me, and over time, we realised that we had many common likes and dislikes and, more importantly, understood and cared about each other. It would not be wrong to admit that I had begun to like and respect her so much that it could only be described as love; her feelings were likewise.

Along with her, I also got to know her friends. Like her, friends too were a bunch of genuine individuals with appreciable qualities, and I interacted with them freely during special occasions, celebrations, and holidays.

Here I would mention a very close friend of Deeti, a lady named Arpana Handa, also a co-worker; a petite young woman, uncomplicated in nature and tastes, resident of

Chennai but shifted to Mumbai. From the beginning itself, both these ladies hit off well. It would not be out of the place to say that one of the prime aims of Deeti, those initial days, was to settle Arpana in this new City which then turned into continuous support to her. And Arpana reciprocated wholeheartedly, always. The mutual regard and love between these two women as it grew always gladdened my heart.

During these days, we three used to meet often, and on one occasion, which happened to be my birthday, Arpana gifted me with an electronic radio clock of a well-known international brand. While profusely thanking her, I expressed my inability to accept such a gift, but she would not listen. Even Deeti was keen that I take the gift, so I relented.

Who was to know that tragedies would strike us soon after and that the radio clock would play such a mysterious role in our lives in the days to come?

That day was the 15th of March, and I had invited Deeti to my residence for dinner. For that reason, I was at home early during the evening. But she was late, and I reckoned that she was delayed at the office. Later in the evening, when the 'grandfather clock' in my drawing-room was showing the time of 8.35 p.m., my doorbell rang. I was expecting her arrival when I opened the door.

I was surprised to see Arpana. Stepping aside with a smile to let her in, I said, "Hello! Please come in. Good to see you. This is the first time you have come to my house. Do sit down."

She walked in slowly and sat down at the corner edge of my only large sofa without returning my smile. She looked agitated. I, too, sat down and looked at her. Was something wrong? Did she have any urgent work with me?

When she spoke, I had difficulty hearing her. She said, "Deeti had an accident in lift number 2 of her building while returning today after office at about 6.45 p.m. I was there and took her to the nearby City hospital. While in deep pain, she just managed to tell me about her evening plan to visit you. At that time, she could not call you as she seemed to have misplaced her mobile phone in the ensuing confusion ... so, on her request, I have personally come to inform you."

That was terrible news, and I said, "What exactly has happened to Deeti? What are the doctors telling you?"

She continued listlessly, "Like I told you, it was a mishap; she tripped and fell headlong inside the lift and hit her head badly. She passed out but then, within seconds, regained consciousness. Luckily, I was waiting outside the lift as it came up to her floor; as the doors opened, I saw her lying in a heap; nobody was in the lift with her. She was feeling extremely sick, so I took her to the hospital; the doctors said there was nothing to worry about and released her after some first aid; I dropped her home. But I fear for the worst! What shall I do?"

There was nothing else she could do or say to me, and then she left. I thought her friend's minor accident had moved her too much. It was unlike her. I was sure Deeti would be alright very soon.

A little later, I called Deeti at her landline number.

When she came on the line, her voice was faint and indistinct.

"So nice of you to call Uttam, but I am..." suddenly, her voice faded away; she appeared very sick.

When I reached her flat without delay, I found that her condition had indeed worsened, although doctors had said not to worry.

Soon she was taken in an ambulance back to the City hospital.

Was Arpana's premonition coming true?

For the next few days, she was in a critical condition, and on the seventh day, I could meet her as a special case.

She looked like a skeleton, having lost considerable weight, and watched me with tired eyes. She wanted to speak, but the words could not come out.

She stayed in the hospital for the next twenty days, but her health was not progressing well. The doctors said that nothing more could be achieved by staying in the hospital and asked her to go home and have personal nursing care.

Even Arpana seemed very unwell these days, and that was understandable; she was so close to her friend.

This was when the unexplained incidents commenced! I had no idea then.

That night in my bed, unexpectedly, my eyes flicked wide open when I heard that the radio of my electronic clock was playing; it was some devotional song. Moments later, it stopped. I lifted my head gingerly and peered at the luminescent radio clock on the side table.

It was showing 2.00 a.m., dead of the night!

I felt annoyed; why did the radio start and stop at this God-forsaken hour? I had not set any radio-alarm.

Then I glanced at the window; it was closed with the curtains drawn together, the AC was working silently, spewing cool air, and the room in the semi-darkness appeared the same when I had switched off the bedside lamp before sleeping.

Thinking that it was of no consequence, I turned on my bed.

Meanwhile, for no reason, I had picked up the radio clock and kept it very near my pillow, subconsciously touching it with the tips of my fingers.

Before long, I felt slightly dizzy and strange, but I closed my eyes again and slept off for how long; I did not know when the radio switched on again, a devotional song started playing, and within seconds became silent. At first, I did not open my eyes for a few moments, but I ventured to look at the radio clock again. That abruptly jerked me out of my sleepiness; what I saw was odd.

The radio clock was showing 12.00 midnight.

That meant the time now was about two hours behind what I had seen last. What was this? Was the clock malfunctioning? Or did I see the time wrong at first, and this was the actual time? Thinking for some moments, I propped up on the bed, switched on the bedside lamp, and picked up my Rolex watch. It was also showing 12.00.

Moving across the pillow, I picked up the radio clock and scrutinised it. There was nothing wrong with it, and it continued to show 12.00 midnight.

Not knowing why, I got up hastily and came out of the bedroom, switched the light in the drawing-room, and looked at the 'grandfather clock'; it was displaying a time of 12.00, the same as I had noticed moments ago.

Somehow, standing there, I felt slightly dizzy and odd again, and my eyes closed for an instant. Was I becoming sick? Was there some confusion in my mind?

At that juncture, I heard noises outside and, opening the main door, found many people were moving around on the street; faintly, I could listen to their shouts, "Earthquake... earthquake...."

I stepped out with alacrity; some people were huddling around at the street corner, talking loudly; they had experienced a significant tremor a little ago, at about 3.45 a.m., and, in fear, had rushed out. Thankfully, there was no damage.

I was surprised. Peculiarly, I had not felt any quake at all.

And more importantly, what about the time?

Just before going out of the house, I saw the time 12.00 midnight. How could the earthquake happen at 3.45 a.m.?

Returning after about five minutes, I again looked at my 'grandfather clock', the radio clock, and checked my Rolex.

Everywhere the time was showing as 4.07 a.m.

Suddenly a tinge of fear started creeping into my consciousness; was there something unexplainable?

The rest of the time, I could not sleep. I repeatedly checked the radio clock, my wristwatch, and the 'grandfather clock'; they were in perfect synchronisation; nothing was wrong anywhere. And compounding this problem was my nagging thought; why did not I experience that earthquake during the night when the rest of the people around felt it so clearly?

A couple of days had passed after that experience. I had returned from my office that evening. Subsequent to my dinner, I was sitting alone and feeling awful. Deeti was in my mind continuously throughout these days, and I could not understand how to help her. Would she live? It seemed difficult by her looks, although the doctors had not given up hope. It was unclear how a mere fall and hit on her head could strike her down so badly. Should I take her to other doctors?

As I was pondering these depressive thoughts, my eyes suddenly fell on the radio clock, and I remembered that night's incident with a mild shudder. I was still unsure what had happened then, even after racking my brain. Was I getting mad? I kept my thoughts to myself.

But oddly, my mind was also veering to the possibility of that incident happening again.

I recalled the night when I was awakened both times by the radio playing, first showing 2.00 a.m., then revealing the 'back time' of 12 midnight.

How? Time did not go in reverse; it only moved forward. The radio clock, I was sure, was working perfectly.

Then, my mind went into overdrive.

I realised that the entire process started and ended with the radio playing.

I also understood that the radio had stopped within seconds in both instances.

The real question was why and what was going on?

Another thought that also played in my mind was, why did I not understand the earthquake that night? The rest of the public did.

An hour had passed when it suddenly struck me that there could be a bizarre reason for all this.

I had physically gone back in time to the past!

Peculiar it might seem, but I was transported back in time through that radio clock device. Was it the stuff of science fiction about time travel?

The radio clock was a Time Machine that took me to the past!

As I thought about it more, the jigsaw puzzle seemed to be getting solved.

Now I realised that when I woke up the first time at 2.00 a.m., which was the actual time, I had started to go back in time, without recognising and in an oblivious state. However, I did feel dizzy and abnormal.

And when I woke up the second time due to the radio playing and saw the time 12 midnight, I was already two hours back in time. Inexplicably, when I had woken up the second time and went to the drawing-room to check, it was a trigger for my return to the actual time, and I again felt dizzy and strange at that time, and my eyes closed momentarily. The whole process happened within minutes without my being any wiser.

Then, it seemed, the actual time was 4.00 a.m. that night, and I had returned to the present time.

Next, I walked out of my house to inquire about the earthquake commotion, and that was another minute or so after 4.00 a.m., and when I returned home after about five minutes, all the clocks and my watch showed the actual time as 4.07 a.m.

I also grasped that when I had gone back in time, the earthquake happened around 3.45 a.m., so I had not felt it.

That was it!

My thoughts were now clear.

This should be confirmed now!

I tentatively picked up the radio clock and checked the current time. It showed the actual time of 9.30 p.m.; I was ready for the bed in my bedroom.

Frowning with silent prayers on my lips, I switched on the radio, and a devotional song started playing.

Somehow, I was profoundly concentrating on going back in time by two hours.

At first, nothing happened, then the radio clock time displays swiftly changed from 9.30 p.m. to 7.30 p.m. and abruptly stopped. The radio, too, stopped playing.

I also felt the familiar slight dizziness, strange, and my eyes closed for an instant.

When my eyes opened, I got up and looked around the house to see if anything had changed and found that it was indeed so; everything indicated that I had just returned from my office, my Rolex watch showed the time of 7.30 p.m., and so did the 'grandfather clock,' and I was feeling hungry. My kitchen lights were switched off, and my briefcase was still on the sofa.

But the radio clock was still in my hand.

Walking out of the house, I surveyed around. There seemed to be no change. The time travel appeared to be happening to me personally, my personal effects, and my immediate surroundings.

I picked up the radio clock and checked the display when I returned to the house. It was still showing at 7.30 p.m. I then switched on the radio and waited. Within a minute or so, the time display changed to the actual time of 9.34 p.m. A song started playing, which abruptly stopped. Once more, this dizziness came...and my eyes closed.

I had returned to the present time!

All this meant that the whole process had happened automatically that night without my understanding and in my sleep, but now I could voluntarily do it. This was in my control through the radio clock!

Now, I needed to do some more experiments.

I tried to go back to some specific date and time in the past, at a familiar place, and found that I could do even that! Interestingly, the Rolex watch I was wearing also travelled with me to the past and showed the new time.

Importantly for all these, I had to keep the radio clock with me, physically.

I was now beginning to have a feeling of exaltation for my new power; how I obtained it, I did not know!

Everything was truly remarkable!

But I was not influenced unnecessarily by these discoveries, and in no time, my thoughts focused on Deeti and the danger she was in.

How could I help her? How can she be saved?

She was critical; I could not let her die when suddenly an idea came into my head! This could be brilliant.

The next day it was late in the evening when I reached Deeti's flat on the 17th floor of a multi-storied building, 'Skyscraper.' It had three lifts, but I took lift number 2 as the other two were not working.

Her house cleaner opened the door. Deeti usually lived alone, but a maidservant and a nurse took care of her continuously after the accident.

She was lying on the bed; her face was pale, and she looked very sick. Seeing me, she gave a wan smile. "Hello, Uttam; what brings you here?" She held out a trembling hand which I held gingerly. She looked worse than what I had last seen. My heart was bleeding for her; I never expected to see her like this.

With a slight quiver in my voice, I said, "Deeti, your health is going down rapidly; I fear for your life... I am very anxious about you... I do not know what to do...."

She softly pulled me close and whispered, "Don't worry, Uttam, I will live, be all right... your love will take care."

I turned away, hiding my tears. "Doctors cannot cure you even after so many days. I have to do something else."

A little later, after making some official mobile calls, I came back and sat on a stool next to her bed and drank tea. I wanted to tell her about my idea. God knew it was a spooky one, but I could try to implement it if she agreed.

I leaned forward and started speaking, "I will tell you about my astonishing experience; this happened after your unfortunate accident. Let me also share how I can take advantage of this experience; who knows, I may be able to help you."

I spoke for the next half an hour; she listened intently; her face showed emotions of surprise and disbelief, but she understood my concern and agreed with me.

The present-day was the evening of the 15th of April, and the time was 6.45 p.m., and I was again in her flat but this time with my radio clock: that Time Machine!

Now was the time to check whether my newfound idea would work or not.

On the 15th of March, last month, I knew that while returning home from the office and after taking lift number 2 of her building at around 6.45 p.m., she had met with that accident. This was said by Deeti's friend, Arpana.

I made her sit up on the bed and held her hand as I had to make her go back with me in time and then, keeping the radio clock on the table, switched on the radio with a silent prayer on my lips. I concentrated intensely on our going back to the past to the day of 15th March, the same time and near lift number 2 of her building. A devotional song started playing on the radio.

Nothing else happened at first, then the song stopped abruptly, but the clock continued to show 6.45 p.m. What was the date?

Soon came the familiar feeling of slight dizziness and the closure of my eyes. The same thing happened to Deeti also.

Opening my eyes almost immediately, I saw that I was transported back in time and was standing near lift number 2 of her building, waiting, when I noticed Deeti was not with me anymore but walking towards me. She was returning from the office that evening, hale and hearty!

This day was the past: the 15th March, and my Rolex wristwatch showed 6.45 p.m. as well.

We were about to start all over again, more so, Deeti!

I greeted her, "So good to see you, Deeti."

She was slightly surprised as she had never expected that I would be waiting there.

"Let us go and have a cup of coffee at the nearby coffee shop." I offered, which she accepted readily.

From her appearance, it was clear that she was unaware of the entire tragic incident which would happen in the immediate future. Not that I expected her to!

So, I did not let her take the lift at 6.45 p.m. That was the danger!

When we came out of the coffee shop, it was 7.57 p.m. As we took lift number 2, it was close to 8.05 p.m. While the lift whirled up smoothly, I looked around. There was nobody except the two of us, and we reached the 17th floor without any incident.

The lift doors opened, and we stepped out; I saw Arpana was standing on the landing, apparently waiting for us.

She smiled, "Good to see you, Deeti. I am happy that you are all right and did not take the lift at 6.45 p.m. I am delighted; all the best to you."

Arpana then looked at me and said, "Your radio clock is lying on the table; please take it and switch on the radio again." With a wave of the hand, she entered the lift, the doors closed silently, and it went down.

As I heard her, I realised with a jolt that I had made a colossal mistake of not carrying the radio clock with me while going back to the past.

But I did not face any problems. The radio clock was thankfully lying on the table when we entered the flat, as Arpana had informed us. I made her sit on the bed.

I switched the radio on, a devotional song started playing, I concentrated, and, in a minute, it stopped; again, that dizziness came, and our eyes closed...!

When our eyes opened instantly, the time on the radio clock had changed to 8.11 p.m., which was tonight, i.e., the 15th of April...!

We were now at the present time, and I observed Deeti keenly; she was still sitting on the bed. But, she looked normal, and there was no sign of any illness. She continued to look hale and hearty as I saw her when returning from office on the 15th of March, while we were in the past.

Now I knew my idea was one of success. I had travelled back with her in time to that fateful day, place, and time and averted her accident by making her take the lift at a later hour. She had avoided the dangerous lift ride at 6.45 p.m. and therefore remained safe.

A couple of nights later, Deeti and I were sitting on the sofa in her flat and celebrating her return to normal health and routine, but there was a doubt in our minds.

I said, "Arpana knew that I had forgotten to take the radio clock with me to the past on the 15th of March, so she advised me that I would find it on the table, but how did she know?"

We deliberated but could not comprehend. The best way was to talk to her and find out.

Deeti said she found out that Arpana was not coming to the office, and the HR department had informed her that Arpana had received sanctioned leave earlier for perhaps going to Chennai, her home City. Deeti would call her later.

As promised, she called Arpana the next day evening after office hours. I was with Deeti in her flat.

There was no reply even after repeated calls.

Deeti said, "I know her parents in Chennai; I will call her mother."

She telephoned, and while she was speaking, her face became ashen, and her hands trembled.

I got up in alarm, "What is happening, Deeti?"

She kept her mobile down and turned towards me with tears in her eyes.

"Arpana had flown to Chennai three nights ago, and later while taking the lift to her parent's flat on the 17th floor of the building, she met with an accident by tripping and hitting her head inside the lift. The name of her multi-storied building in Chennai is 'Tower,' which indicates the same name as my building, 'Skyscraper,' the floor number is similar, the 17th and the time of her accident were also alike, 6:45 p.m. This was the time I also had my accident."

She gulped and again started.

"After Arpana's mishap, there was considerable delay in getting help; ultimately, her parents found her unconscious inside the lift. Curiously, no one else had used the lift during that period. Now she is in the hospital fighting for her life."

We were utterly stunned! Mystified! Her accident was uncannily comparable to the misfortune of Deeti!

We wanted to fly to Chennai to be at her side. I also thought about taking that radio clock with me; perhaps I could save her the way I had saved Deeti. Tragically the instrument had become nonfunctional by then, totally lifeless, so to speak.

Only we could not be at her side. An hour later, we got the sad news about her death!

In the end, Arpana left behind many unanswered questions, but we knew that in some supernatural way, she had saved Deeti's life through that paranormal Time Machine cum radio clock in exchange for her own life.

We were reminiscing with tears in our eyes; she was a perfectly normal human without special powers, but ultimately proved to be an incredible friend in an extraordinary manner!

CHAPTER SIX

EERIE WORDS

Devaa Bhutani was feeling stressed. It was psychological, not due to any physical ailment. He was a sturdy young man with an impressive build.

During the day, he went through the routines of attending his college classes, returning to his room later in the evening, and completing his dinner without much ado. Nonetheless, he could not place his finger on the precise reason for his discomfiture.

That night he opened his red diary to jot down his thoughts and incidents of the day, as was his daily habit for many years. On skimming through its pages, he randomly opened a page of twenty-three days ago - the 20th of January, on which he had penned:-

'I will surely flunk my test for the physics paper; my preparation is unbelievably bad.'

He recalled, after this writing, that he had tried to prepare himself properly. He was generally a good and confident student; he knew that his attempt had been satisfactory.

It was a shock when he received his marks yesterday; he had failed miserably. In some way, he looked to have anticipated the failure on the 20th of January itself by writing in the diary. And that had come true! Possibly this fact was flirting in his subconscious mind, making him anxious.

However, he believed that this unlucky prediction was only a coincidence.

About a month later, Devaa went to Patna, where his parents stayed. He was on the train - Himgiri Express, and it was night. As was his habit, he wrote in his daily diary:-

'Feeling so happy to visit my parents. Not informing them. Afraid they may not be at home. But still.'

He meant the visit to be a surprise. He knew that his parents did not travel often. But it was not expected that his words would result in another happenstance. The following day when he arrived home, he found that his parents were not there. They had left for the adjoining town last night to visit his grandmother, who unexpectedly had a heart attack. He was unaware since they could not contact him over the mobile phone – some connectivity problems prevailed while he was on the train.

Then, almost a week had gone by, and Devaa was back in Kolkata. He had managed to meet his parents later and visit his grandmother, but somehow, he did not dismiss the incident, which looked to be linked with what he recorded in his diary.

Another night, before going to bed, he had written in his diary:-

'I am short of money. Hope parents will send me at-least Rs. 15000/-. Need to speak to them.'

The following day there was a wire transfer of the exact sum in his bank account done by his father. He had never uttered his need to his parents.

This was odd; it looked to be another fluke.

Next month, it was that day when Devaa was terribly upset with his mathematics lecturer. Not for the first time that the gentleman tried to make Devaa's life difficult in class. His misbehaviour had been extreme; Devaa was made a laughing stock before his classmates.

During the night, Devaa penned in his diary, with a deep sense of frustration:-

'Such a terrible day in college. *Do not know why Deep Sir is badly humiliating me. I hope he suffers also. Teach him a lesson.*'

The incident did not stop with that diary noting.

Two days afterwards, the entire college was surprised to know that Deep Sir was entangled in an embezzlement and cheating case; it was a huge embarrassment for him.

Was it one more quirk?

These four coincidences or flukes, whatever one could describe, in some way, shook Devaa considerably. What was really happening? Did the red diary play any role here? He wanted to verify his doubts.

That night he sat on his bed thinking. He would check his misgivings now. His sixth sense told him that something would occur; a sensation of melancholy was also creeping in.

There was load shedding, and the whole neighbourhood was in darkness. A candle was burning on his table in his small room, intermittently flickering with the soft breeze wafting through the open window. Eerie lights and shades were moving on the walls. The entire environment gave a negative impression.

With a strong will, Devaa opened his diary and started writing on the page of the day:-

"Feeling depressed...," he stopped and thought - what else could he write? Perhaps a friend would be welcome at this time to lift his mood. His instinct was telling him to call Parul. He decided that he would do so after completing the diary for the day. Then he wrote, *'I want Parul; I hope she will show up now.'*

Parul Verma was his classmate in the City college who stayed not too far away in a girl's hostel.

After writing in the diary, he waited pensively. What would happen next?

Just then, he heard a knock on the door. It was now the moment of truth; his legs felt weak and unsteady beneath him. Getting up slowly, he unlatched the lock and opened the door. The landing outside was in some darkness, slightly lit up from the illumination of the candle, enough to recognise the person.

That was Parul, all right!

Devaa's heart missed a beat. This meant the red diary was converting his wish into reality!

Seeing him, Parul smiled and entered the room. "Oh, my goodness! You look so scared, Devaa. Have you not seen me before? Do I look like a ghost?"

She walked past him and sat on the chair.

Even in that dim light, she looked beautiful. The two had started to share an intimate relationship bordering on love quite recently. It was not so easy. Some months back, Devaa and Parul often seriously quarrelled on many topics. Their bitterness was the talk amongst their friends in those days. Many friends did not know that subsequently, they had patched up so well.

Seeing Devaa standing near the door immobilised, she beckoned to him, "Oh, come on, close the door. Sorry to annoy you so belatedly in the night, but suddenly I felt like coming to you."

She tossed her hair back and gave a bright smile. That broke the spell, and he could breathe freely. The electricity supply resumed as he closed the door, and the room was lit up. The entire foreboding atmosphere just melted off.

But Devaa was still worried. He silently picked up the diary and looked at his lines, written just some minutes ago, then at Parul. Was this the fifth happenstance he had just created by writing in his diary? Was this diary a method through which he could control his surroundings? Only this was entirely supernatural; nobody in their right senses would believe him.

Despite that, he had to confide in somebody; he needed some other viewpoint, some advice. Somehow, a hidden fear was slowly engulfing him.

Looking at Parul, he swiftly made up his mind. Putting water to boil in a kettle for tea, he sat on the bed and marshalled his thoughts on how he would begin his bizarre tale.

"Parul...," he hesitated for a few seconds, "I have some very odd things to tell you; believe me, not a single word will be false; everything I say will be nothing but the facts...."

Parul stared at him.

He continued, "For the last few months, I have noticed that too many coincidences are happening in my life, and frighteningly, those have occurred after I have written about them in my diary." Taking out his diary and opening the appropriate pages, he explained the incidents in great detail, omitting nothing; at the end, saying, "The last one had come about just a while ago when I wrote - wanting your presence. And here you are...." He showed the day's page.

All this time, Parul had listened without interruption. Gradually a sense of surprise was building up, as was evident from her face. When he stopped, she got up, refraining from giving any comments but shaking her head in disbelief, prepared two cups of tea, and returned.

"What you told me just now is absolutely crazy, nobody will believe you, but I trust you." Sipping the tea, she spoke supportively and touched him lightly on his face. "We all know that many things that happen in this world are unexplainable, but that does not mean that they have no existence, so we should agree that there is something supernatural in that diary. Let us think about where we need to go from here."

She kept her eyes on him, whose teacup was untouched. It was clear that Parul was unwilling to let Devaa panic unnecessarily.

Devaa, though perplexed, seemed to be taking control of himself and was slowly getting an answer; his thought process was expanding somehow into the realm of the unknown.

He picked up the diary and opened the first page. "This red diary was gifted to me by our friend Chintan Garg last December. His salutation is here. He also gave me a pen to write in the diary. We know that Chintan, a very mercurial and short-tempered guy with suspected bipolar mental illness, had died under mysterious conditions of cyanide poisoning. He was probably killed because someone might have forced him to use cyanide; the police are still investigating the matter...." Then he stopped. "Could there be a connection between him and the incongruous quality of that diary?"

Devaa got into intense thoughts, and Parul remained silent, frowning deeply.

Coming out of his reverie, he said, "If so, then I ask, why had all these events occurred? Since his death was unnatural, a murder, perhaps the spirit of Chintan wants his killer to be found out through this spectral diary? And does he want me to do that?"

He looked up at Parul questioningly and continued, "Does it make any sense?"

Parul appeared pensive and said, "Probably, but I do not believe in ghosts and unknowns."

Both Devaa and Parul could not fathom their next course of action that night.

A week had since elapsed, during which Devaa's mind was perpetually in turmoil. His intellect repeatedly lingered on the supernatural diary; moreover, he had stopped writing anything in it. He did not know how long this state of affairs would continue and what he should do.

That was when the incident happened.

In the late afternoon, Devaa was returning from college; the classes were over; he was riding his motorcycle, and he planned to visit the gym in the evening. It was the usual traffic. But then, suddenly, a car coming from the opposite direction swerved while he was about to cross it. It hit him; he was thrown out and landed a few feet away on the cemented sidewalk. An intense flash of light before his eyes and unbearable pain shot through his body before a curtain of darkness enveloped him. There were shouts from people around, and they rushed towards him. In the melee, the car driver escaped through the adjoining narrow lanes.

When Devaa regained consciousness in the hospital and opened his eyes, the face which came into his vision was that of Parul. She touched his forehead lovingly and said, "Thank goodness you are OK...." The doctor standing next to her checked Devaa and told her that he would recover soon, but rest and regular medication needed to be ensured.

As hours passed, Devaa could think coherently; he could strangely recall certain atypical events when he became unconscious moments after the accident; this had to be told. Since his mouth was turning dry at this time, he could not speak to Parul. Weakly, he just managed to say, "I must tell you something, but before that, give me some water...."

Little later, with Parul standing near him, he spoke, barely whispering, "When I met with the accident, initially, for a moment, everything went blank with agonising pain, then slowly a blurred vision came that somebody was standing before me telling me something. You would not believe it - he was Chintan! His lips were moving wordlessly, and he was pointing towards a red diary he was holding in his left hand ... his entire expression was as if he wanted me to do something. He then moved his finger across his throat as if suggesting something violent..., perhaps was trying to take advantage of my distressed mind."

Devaa stopped, out of breath, closed his eyes, and muttered, "After that, I do not remember anything; I woke up in this hospital."

Parul ran her fingers through his hair with a worried look and said soothingly, "Now relax and get well; we will sort this out later."

Devaa was extremely fortunate that he had survived.

The following week he was discharged from the hospital. Doctors told him that his fractured left elbow would take time to mend.

About a month and a half had passed since then. Devaa was almost healed. In his room, with Parul at his side, they were talking. It was afternoon already.

Devaa was saying, "For many days, I had thought about my weird experience, and I seem to be getting a clear message that the ghost of Chintan wants me to take help of the diary to know who murdered him... and perhaps punish his killer."

"But," Parul said, "... how are you so sure?" She had doubts about it.

Devaa said, "I have an idea to check if my line of thinking is correct." He picked up the diary, thought for some moments, and wrote on the page the current date:-

'Chintan's killer will surrender to the local police station at 5.15 p.m. today.'

Parul, too, was looking at those words with a puckered brow.

He said, "I know your uncle works there as a sub-inspector. Will you please ask him to tell if anybody surrenders around that time?"

She nodded slightly.

During the late evening, Parul again visited Devaa.

On entering his room, she stated, "My uncle informed me that no one has surrendered to the police. So, now?"

Devaa remained quiet for many minutes, then said, "This means that Chintan was not killed by anybody. Otherwise, the killer would have surrendered. I somehow trust in the mysterious power of the diary. So, nobody poisoned him."

He paused and then went on, "What could have actually happened? There are two options; either his death was due to an accident or a suicide. Cyanide poison is hazardous; it cannot be accidentally obtained and consumed. But it seemed that Chintan had managed to buy it surreptitiously and could have deliberately consumed it. So, am I to believe that he had committed suicide?"

Devaa stopped and looked at Parul, "My next question is – why did he do that?"

He was surprised to see tears in Parul's eyes for the first time. She hastily wiped them and went up to have a drink of water. She said, "Yes...that is the question...why?" Stopping abruptly, she turned her face away. She could not venture to say anything further; her face expressed extreme unease when she turned.

Somehow, Devaa felt in his bones that she was concealing something. This was a matter of grave importance to him, and he would like to know the truth. But how? There could be a solution to that. He excused himself and went out of the room, closing the door behind him. The diary was in his pocket. Once outside, he wrote in his diary:-

'Now, I will come to know why Chintan had committed suicide.'

He re-entered his room.

"I must tell you, Devaa, what happened before Chintan's death." He noticed that Parul was about to reveal something and knew that the power of the red diary was working.

"That fateful day, hours before Chintan committed suicide, I was in his room. Suddenly, he told me that he wanted me, loved me, and yearned for me physically. I was thunderstruck, and before I could react, he lunged towards me to tear my clothes and perhaps rape me... he was totally weird ... maniac!" With a broken voice, she was speaking.

She interrupted herself for a few moments with tears that still overwhelmed her eyes.

"I had to save myself that day; I tried to hold him, reasoned with him, refused him, I said I did not love him.

He was not listening and progressively became very violent and full of hate. I slapped him to stop and then left his room, saying that I would never have anything to do with him, let alone marry him. While going out, I heard him screaming and threatening me that he would get at me at any cost...take revenge for refusing him!"

She stopped and looked away for a moment.

"That day, he became so vicious and deserved to be halted. But trust me, I do not know why this incident made him commit suicide."

Devaa was not aware of these facts, and the revelation shook him. Chintan was his close friend, but he had never known that Chintan had any criminal desire for Parul, their mutual friend. But what was that about retribution?

His mind was unwilling to think more. Confusion prevailed!

Then, an extrasensory missive hit him like lightning out of the blue. He swore an oath beneath his breath, took out the diary from his pocket, and looked through the pages. Mysteriously, on the last page, twelve handwritten words had appeared out of nowhere, evidently written by Chintan, whose handwriting Devaa recognised. This fortified Devaa's blurred vision of Chintan, who was trying to give him a message just after Devaa's accident.

Chintan's horrific handwritten words read, "KILL PARUL. PUT ME AT PEACE! SHOW NO MERCY - MY DEAR FRIEND!"

The picture now cleared remarkably! A direct communiqué!

The ghost of Chintan wanted Devaa to take vengeance against Parul!

It was incredible but true! Parul was not at fault; her only failing was that she did not yield to the lecherous desires of Chintan. Her rejection made him a jilted lover, which had triggered this criminal emotion, together with his shameless desire.

The red diary that Chintan gifted to Devaa sometime before his death was supernaturally converted into deceased Chintan's weapon in Devaa's hands. The diary had given unusual powers to Devaa by which he could commit a crime of revenge against Parul on behalf of Chintan.

Chintan, however, did not say how Devaa would have to kill Parul and, most importantly, why!

Perhaps Chintan thought that the earlier bitter relationship between Devaa and Parul, all friends were aware, would smoothen the passage of this crime. Chintan did not know that both had patched up later and now shared an intimate relationship bordering on love.

But supposing that even though there was no love between Devaa and Parul and only resentment, why would Devaa become a criminal for Chintan and take revenge? Curiously, the answer might be found in Chintan's treacherously twisted passion. He was already a guy suspected of bipolar mental illness, which made him think that Devaa as a close friend, would support his abnormal passion, which had turned to seek revenge on a defenceless and mistreated woman. And that paranormal mindset continued in Chintan even after his death, in his unearthly existence!

Indeed, this world was a weird place!

As these horrific thoughts swept through his mind, the foremost concern became how to save himself and Parul?

"It is so sad that Chintan has threatened you before his death, but those were not hollow words for him. Through this ghostly diary, he wanted me to take his revenge on you in whatever way would be most ruthless." He said.

Listening to all these perils was too much for Parul; she bent down and covered her face sobbing uncontrollably as he continued.

Almost an hour passed in this way. Both Devaa and Parul did not speak a single word. There were grave unearthly threats! They had to find a way out of this. Who or what could help them?

This diary? The sources of all problems or solutions?

At that instant, an unbelievable idea struck him! Devaa picked up the diary and wrote on the day's page:-

'I want the spirit of Chintan to attain eternal peace of mind and all his thoughts of revenge to go forever.'

Would this be the masterstroke to get out of this mysterious danger? Was the diary more potent than its malicious originator?

It became apparent in no time.

Soon after writing these words, a subconscious flood of relief passed through his mind, as if a tremendous mental burden had lifted and vanished. Parul echoed a similar sentiment. "It is as if we are receiving a fresh lease of life. Thank goodness!" She uttered.

Then, a sudden flash of light happened so swiftly and robust that they momentarily closed their eyes. Another transformation was happening before their gaze! The red diary was changing its colour to green, translucent green.

Astounding!

"My God! Enough of this nonsense. Please get rid of this dangerous diary." Parul exclaimed.

No more words were needed. Only, how was he do that?

Devaa again picked up the diary and wrote.

'I am sure the spirit of Chintan will not mind if this diary gets lost or destroyed.'

Nothing out of the ordinary happened that night.

The next afternoon, Devaa was returning from college. The diary was in his trouser pocket. Parul was with him. On the way, there was a sudden torrential downpour. He stopped the motorcycle, and both took shelter under a tree. It was crowded with many people jostling with each other to save themselves.

When the rain subsided, they decided to go to the nearest coffee shop. While sitting at the table, they noticed that the diary was missing from his pocket.

It was lost forever.

Just then, Parul got a call from her sub-inspector uncle. "You have been enquiring about the investigation of Chintan's death. Today, the police have closed the matter; it is a case of suicide only."

Parul put her hand over Devaa's; he reciprocated.

Then, one of those days, he decided to buy another diary to continue his habit of writing every day. Entering his room, he sat down to write in his new diary. He picked up the pen Chintan had gifted him along with that cursed diary.

With that red diary gone, he started writing in his new diary with a sense of relief:-

'Feeling happy today. Want to enjoy this evening with Parul.'

Subsequently, he relaxed in the chair with a book after changing his clothes. He would request her, a little later, to come.

Though that was not done, at around 6.45 p.m., unexpectedly, he heard a knock on the door. Parul was standing at the doorway, looking pretty in a fashionable dress, ready for an outing.

"I believe you want me. Here I am! Shall we have dinner together this evening?" She said, smiling.

Devaa was taken aback; how could he still convert his wish into reality? But the bizarre diary was gone!

Minutes afterwards, nevertheless, he realised. It was Chintan's pen, with which he had been writing his diary all these months; so, both the diary and the pen were spooky!

Realising this, he wondered, would the ghostly problem be revealed again?

"No," Parul said, "the ghost of Chintan is now at peace, remember."

She was so right; nevertheless, he had to get rid of the pen that evening itself.

CHAPTER SEVEN

DOUBT OR NOT TO DOUBT

It was late winter afternoon when I entered the small hutment situated just on the sides of a large pond with tranquil and clear water surrounded by trees and shrubs all around its periphery. A small window, bare and half-broken, was overlooking that water body. While entering, my mind was somewhat apprehensive. Shaanu Sengupta, my dear friend, was at my side, whose hand I caught then with a vice grip; my palm was cold as I held him.

He looked at me with a smile, "Do not be afraid, Gauri; all you hear about this pond and this area from the villagers are *bunkum*. We will prove that there is nothing supernatural here. Staying one night here is sufficient."

Darshan Majhi, the head villager, standing just outside the door, stepped inside with a serious face. "Sir, please do not take this place lightly; there is something ghostly here that cannot be explained by anyone. For years, this has been going on, and many people confirmed this extraordinary phenomenon."

"Can you once again explain in detail why all you villagers are so scared about this hutment and the pond?" asked Shaanu.

I did not want to hear all these a second time, but Darshan was willing to repeat the incidents again.

According to him, in 2016, a middle-aged gentleman named Karan Goswami came from Kolkata to this village, 'Ram-Gaon,' in the Munger district of the State of Bihar, to study flora and fauna; he was a biologist. While scouting around the adjoining areas of this village, he came across this pond situated around two kilometers to the west, inside the forest. The hutment was also there, most probably constructed decades ago by the British, who had also developed this area to unwind and fish.

One Sunday afternoon, Karan told Darshan that he intended to go to that region for fishing and stay overnight to examine nature at night. Since he knew about an old electricity cable connecting the hutment to the village's central electric transmission tower, he wanted to see if it was still functioning. That was, and so Karan Goswami left for the pond with a fishing pole and other gears.

The following day, when he failed to return to the village, Darshan Majhi, with two of his friends, went to find out what had happened. There, they met with a totally unexpected sight. Karan Goswami was lying on the floor, unconscious. With some difficulty, he was moved to the main hospital about five kilometers from the village in the nearest district town, and he recovered after several days of hospitalization.

On inquiry by the local police, he could only say that night he had heard perplexing noises of splashing in the pond as if there was some supernatural large-sized creature in the waters. And this repeatedly happened whenever he switched the electric light on inside the hutment to try to see the cause of the noise correctly. The same noise was heard when he switched the light off. Initially, he went out in the darkness near the pond to check but was clueless. By and by, he became so scared in that faraway place inside the deep forest that he lost his senses. He never remembered anything after that.

With this incident, fear developed around this area, and in general, the villagers avoided going to this side of the forest.

A year later, a young man named Hemendra Ghosh came to the village to investigate the strange incident. He was a friend of Karan Goswami's son and had learned about the incident from him. After staying overnight, he also harboured the same impression that there were ghostly creatures inside the pond that nobody saw in the daytime, but one could experience them during late nights.

That second visit and reaffirmation of the inexplicable occurrences inside the pond created a further fear psychosis and seldom had anyone visited there for the last many years.

Then another unrelated incident happened last year, during the winter. An old woman was found dead by drowning in that pond! When her rotting dead body was discovered in the water a week later by a couple of farmers who were traversing that area at a distance, it was believed to be a mishap. She would have wandered away inside the forest near the pond during darkness, missed her steps and plunged into the water. The odd thing was that she was totally an unknown woman, and someone remembered that she had alighted from a train from Kolkata a day earlier. Eventually, the police failed to identify her, and she was cremated after a few days with Hindu rituals. That could have been the end of the matter; however, some villagers doubted that she was a victim of those ghostly creatures.

That late winter afternoon, Shaanu and I were in that area to investigate that incident we had heard from the 'Seekers of Ghosts Club' in Kolkata. Shaanu, although interested in the supernatural and ghosts, he firmly believed that all these were figments of the imagination of pathetic minds, and he had to prove that. There were no ghosts!

But I was not so sure. For centuries, people had experienced ghosts and paranormal activities, and considerable research and investigation continued. While there were never any authoritative findings, I kept my options open, and I was worried about the unknowns.

As I looked intently at the expanse of the pond water in the fading sun and the shadows of the greenery reflecting on the water, there was nothing to be frightened of. The inside of the hutment was in a disused state with semi-concrete broken floor and walls with peeling and ruptured paint and plaster. The lone electric bulb was just across the open window on the opposite wall, and when I tried to switch it on, it worked.

We settled in, and eventually, at 9.45 p.m., after a frugal dinner, we both tried to be comfortable on the floor with a mat rolled out while sharing a warm blanket to keep the cold out. The single bulb was burning brightly, must be 200 watts, lighting up the small room as if there was sunlight; the rays of the bulb were percolating out and visible from outside the hutment through the cracks of the door and the single open window overlooking the pond. The darkness outside, with no moon, formed an overarching black cover; the virtually invisible tall trees nearby, with rustling noise, accentuated the environment. Shaanu went out to make a reconnaissance of the area, and on return, he shook his head and said, "I was practically blind as bat outside; the only exception is that the light leaking out the hutment makes it seem to be an alien structure sitting on the ground. There is no movement of the pond's water, which is perfectly natural in this windless weather, and I would say that all these ghost fears inside the water are bogus."

I said nothing, especially since I felt a constant tremor of fear in myself. Shaanu was nonchalant; an adventurous feeling was the dominant attitude for him.

We found nothing amiss as we tried to keep awake. I reckoned my eyes were gradually closing due to sleep when we heard a noise in the pond. Shaanu was on full alert right away, and we sat up, trying to look outside the window. Nothing was heard after that.

Shaanu waited for some time after saying in a low tone that we should switch off the light; perhaps whoever was outside was repelled by the light. Even the experience of other men here had pointed to a particular link with the light.

He got up and switched off the light, and almost immediately, we heard a loud splash in the pond. We moved near the window and checked, but we could see nothing other than dark waters. Then he nodded at me, I moved back, switched on the light, and then there was another splash noise; dimly, we could see that the water was moving with significant ripples. Shaanu stared at the scene for some moments and indicated to switch off the light again. There was another noise; next, I put on the light again of my own volition and, after counting a few seconds, put it off, causing repetitions of the noise in the pond.

Almost immediately, it was becoming clear to us that no supernatural activity was happening here. The reason was straightforward; the pond was full of fishes, small and large, and in the absolute darkness, the intensely bright light of the electric bulb was falling on the water like a burning spear attracting the fishes. Therefore, as soon as the light was switched off, the school of fish drawn to that spot of light moved away, creating a splash, and as the light was switched on, those fishes jumped back towards the spot, making another, stronger, splash. Thus, there was a perfectly natural reason for which no cause of fear could arise.

The next day, after we explained the phenomenon to the villagers, the pond and the natural surroundings of the hutment ceased to become a place of terror to them, and we prepared to return the same day to Kolkata.

While this was the end of our ghost investigation in this part of Bihar, I remembered that before leaving in the afternoon, when I was still inside the hutment, alone, packing a few things, I heard a noise of very loud splashing in the pond. While looking out, I could see nothing. The pond was so tranquil, as if there was no splash of fish at any time. Thinking that my imagination was going wild, I refrained from raising this subject before Shaanu, who had gone ahead towards the village.

Later, Shaanu became more emboldened to say that there were no ghosts or any supernatural activities and all such experiences by various people over the years had natural or logical causes, even weak hearts. Even though I had to agree reluctantly at that time, my fears did not leave me. I did not want him to get into another paranormal environment where he could get into trouble. I loved him too much and could not afford to lose him.

Almost three months had passed after we returned from that village, 'Ram-Gaon,' when Shaanu's passion for proving that supernatural or ghosts did not exist reared its head again. This time it was a mansion just outside the city limits, which had decades of the reputation of being haunted. Stories abounded; it was difficult to understand what exactly made this place creepy.

As usual, there was no way I could talk him out of it. So, we made the plan to visit the mansion, stay the night and prove that there was nothing like a ghost.

That Sunday late evening, I entered the gates of the dilapidated ageless mansion with a certain apprehension. Shaanu had already gone in.

The fading sunlight played hide & seek in the edifice in various nooks and corners, pathways, broken down veranda, staircases, and all around the mansion. The inside from the doorway looked dark and forlorn. The inner view from a few scattered windows presented the same picture. For miles, the overgrown trees and shrubs surrounding the structure depicted closed, forbidding, and scary greenery!

I looked around. Shaanu, too, was surveying the area.

"This place has something frightening I can feel in my bones," I said. "Moreover, there is no electricity here."

"So what? Do not jump to conclusions. Let the night pass." Shaanu said loudly; he was in his usual disbelieving self, more so after the incident in that village.

There was another reason for his being aggressive about this visit. There was a stormy argument in the college cafeteria the day before with one of his friends. "There is no ghost ... ever," were his final words, "... no more arguments. We will prove it tomorrow!" Shaanu had said.

"But," his friend Rohit had smiled, "it is well known that you will never see one if you go looking for ghosts."

That evening we were prepared for the night. The sun was going down fast; a long night was coming.

We entered the mansion through the main door, cleared the cow webs, kept handkerchiefs on our noses to ward off the dust of God knows how many years, walked through numerous rooms, corridors, and corners, negotiated a few flying bats, and ultimately found a small room which had only one door but was relatively clean.

We settled in for a long wait.

"How long do you reckon?" I looked at Shaanu.

"Your guess is as good as mine. God Knows." He seemed dismissive. The darkness was by then absolute, night insects were making noises, and the night seemed to be taking its grip. The atmosphere was getting more and more ominous. Our one flickering candle looked like it was fighting a lost battle.

Some hours must have passed; we were dozing off, not strictly keeping a tab on time, when suddenly we heard a low moan! It was as though somebody was suffering pain.

We were immediately alert, looked at each other, and got up after a silent nod. With our torches switched on, we took our bearings and moved.

Shaanu was at the front.

We paused, crossing a long corridor and coming near a room where the low moan appeared to be permeating. The door was partly open, but it was inky dark inside.

Shaanu pushed the creaking door in and flicked the flashlight beam around.

I gritted my teeth, my heart was palpitating painfully, I felt short of breath, and sweat formed on my forehead.

God knows how Shaanu was feeling.

At first, we witnessed nothing, but the moving light caught a glimpse of someone lying on the ground in the far corner. Turning the light, an old woman with a white sheet covered up her chin came into our view. Her snow-white hair contrasted with the darkness. Her pinched-up thin face was the most pathetic sight, showing despair and deep pain.

She groaned once more.

We moved swiftly into action.

"Who are you? What happened?" Shaanu touched her forehead. "My God, she is burning with fever."

The old woman muttered, "Please help me...I think I'm dying ... give me water." She started gasping for breath.

I ran out of the room towards our room to fetch the water bottle.

When I came back, Shaanu was kneeling at the woman's side, holding her gnarled thin hand.

I opened the bottle and gently poured water into her mouth. She abruptly shuddered and closed her eyes; her frail body became still!

I reached for her pulse and felt her nostrils; there was no beat, no breath. The poor woman had died! Shaanu, too, checked after giving a little gap to ensure this fact.

Her body was ice cold! So was her tattered wet saree.

"What should we do now?" I looked at Shaanu with trepidation.

It was something we never expected.

"Let us not waste any time; this woman is dead; we must do something...inform the police."

I nodded, and we came out of the mansion, carefully finding our way through the darkness, and reached my car, parked nearby.

Before that, I had taken a photo of the poor dead woman from my mobile camera; it was on an impulse.

Shaanu said, "She is human; now you know there are no ghosts. This mansion is just a relic with beggars occupying it over the years, and their movements made people think this was haunted. And you find another destitute dying of hunger and disease."

"But," I said, "one can argue like this; the old woman may not have anything to do with ghosts, but this mansion could still be haunted."

"All rubbish!" Shaanu retorted loudly. "Let somebody convince me ... I challenge anybody." He sneered.

I did not like this attitude but kept quiet.

When we reached the nearest police station, it was 2.30 a.m., and very few personnel were there, but we managed to convince the in-charge to go to the mansion. The photo of that dead woman on my mobile phone could not be ignored by them.

The police said that they would act and asked us to go home.

It was a long drive entering the City; an hour later, I dropped Shaanu near his hostel gate and drove off to my house, thinking of the unexpected anti-climax to our search for ghosts.

The following day, I was awakened by my mobile ringing. It was bright and sunny, and the time was 10.20 a.m. I was acutely late due to our night adventure.

The call was from one Inspector Rathod, whom I remembered we met during the night. "Ma'am, you should at once come to the police station." He seemed disturbed.

Before I started, I gave a call to Shaanu, but there was no response. I was sure he was still sleeping. Deciding not to disturb him in his hostel, I went to my car.

After another long drive, I reached the police station and walked into the room of Rathod; he seemed restless.

"What is the problem?" I looked at him feeling slightly troubled. The police were not supposed to get agitated.

Rathod sat down. "Ma'am, You know whom we found when we went to that old mansion around 6.00 a.m. today after you and your friend came to us?"

I stared at him.

"There was no old woman in that room, dead or alive; instead, your friend's unconscious body was lying there! We have shifted him to the local hospital. But I thought both of you had gone home. Who removed the dead body? What sort of complexity is this?"

I continued to gaze at him and could not believe what I had heard; my head reeled, and I sat shakily on the nearby bench.

Soon I got up and reached the hospital to find that Shaanu was recovering; he was conscious. Inspector Rathod had accompanied me.

As I smoothened his forehead, he looked at me with a weak smile.

"How are you feeling, Shaanu? What is this strange happening? You were in your hostel last night. Why did you go to the mansion? What the hell is going on with that dead old woman?" I asked.

"You will not believe what I will say...," Shaanu replied in a low tone, quite unlike his robust behaviour. "After you dropped me at the hostel and I had gone off to sleep, I dreamt about that old woman asking me to go to an apartment at the rear of some hospital; I could see that apartment building and its door in my dream. When I woke up or regained my senses as per the doctors, I found myself in this hospital, which I think is the same one that the old woman was telling me about. I do not remember leaving my hostel at any time... I know nothing else."

At this time, Inspector Rathod explained the facts to him. Soon Shaanu became reticent and, with a sigh, said, "Everything ... so very weird, I do not know, I feel very shaken, scared...." He stopped and took my hand, which was trembling.

Two days had since passed after that tragedy; after getting discharged from the hospital, Shaanu and I searched for that apartment building which we found quickly enough.

It was afternoon when we climbed the rickety stairs of the building and rang the doorbell of that apartment.

Moments later, a middle-aged lady opened the door and looked at us inquiringly. It was very awkward for me to explain why we were there, but instinctively I took out my mobile phone and showed her the photo of that dead woman. As that lady looked at the photo, her eyes moistened, and she started swaying but supported herself by holding the door.

"Who are you? How did you get this photo? What do you want?" Her voice was shaky.

"Can we come in?" I asked.

Soon we were sitting in the minuscule ramshackle drawing-room.

When Shaanu ended his short and astonishing narrative, that lady, whose name was Jharna Dutt and standing before us, started weeping silently.

I stood up and gently coaxed her to sit down.

By and by, she controlled herself and told us her part of the tale. It was heart-wrenching.

The photo of the dead woman was that of her maternal grandmother. Her name was Sulochona Devi. The grandfather had died long ago, and even Jharna's parents were no more. Besides, Jharna was a spinster, and no other living relatives existed

So, there were only Sulochona Devi and Jharna, who lived together in that apartment for many years, happily.

Unfortunately, last year, these two ladies had some difference of opinion, which became so severe that one afternoon, Sulochona Devi left home in great annoyance without informing her granddaughter. After that, Jharna tried to trace her but in vain. Soon, her remorse knew no bounds, and she went into a depression. She could never forget the mutual love and affection they had shared since her childhood. How could a minor turmoil bring about such a drastic step? She was sure that her grandmother would realise her folly and return to her; she loved her too much. But that was not happening!

When we arrived today, her emotional state was apparent while we showed her the grandmother's photo and told her this incredible tale!

In the end, she could not bring about to think that her grandmother was dead. Even if Jharna acknowledged that demise, repeatedly she asked why she could not see her physical body; did she not die only recently? The mysterious disappearance of the body was not acceptable. The police should be able to track her down. Many questions remained unanswered. We felt it was our responsibility to sort out the unknowns.

That evening itself, we visited Inspector Rathod. While I was briefing him on our visit to the granddaughter, I had a couple of premonitions.

Was there a connection between this dead woman in the mansion and what we heard about the death in the forest of 'Ram-Gaon'? I recalled Darshan Majhi had said that an old woman was found dead by drowning in that pond! She was not a local woman and had come from Kolkata. Ultimately, she had remained unidentified by the police after the investigation. So, could they have kept any record, including a photo of that woman?

And finally, what about my odd experience while leaving this village? To bring to mind, when I was going away from that hutment, I heard a noise of very loud splashing in the pond. What was it that I had tried to ignore? Was that the supernatural signal of that old woman falling into the pond and dying?

The inspector was helpful and promised to do whatever possible to sort out these queries.

Later, when we again visited Jharna's tiny apartment, I had the photo of the unidentified dead woman, taken by the police in that village after fishing her out of the pond but before cremation. It was not a pleasant sight, but her face was unmistakable.

When Jharna saw that police photo and again the mobile phone photo, I took while in the mansion, which matched, she broke down completely! She was convinced! The old woman who drowned was indeed her grandmother, who had reached 'Ram-Gaon' in a fit of anger and unfortunately met her death, probably accidentally. And her apparition was seen by us in that dilapidated ageless mansion; in fact, she wanted that!

Here we understood one reality very clearly. Even after death, deep love and affections had prevailed; otherwise, why would she want to connect with her granddaughter from the ethereal world? Providentially we were made the mystical medium between these two 'SHEs'!

Shaanu was now a reluctant believer of unknowns, and justifiably so!